A HORROR NOVELLA

CHADBOURNE

WILLIAM F. GRAY

Praise for NORO

NORO is seriously dread-inducing. I hit a point where I didn't want to turn the page, but I HAD TO. This novella is wildly cinematic, fast-paced, bloody, and slicing cold. I'd give it comp titles, but I went in blind and you'll be grateful you did, too. Dog lovers be warned, though!! This one'll break your heart and make you squirm."

— Sam Rebelein, Bram Stoker-nominated author of EDENVILLE and THE POORLY MADE AND OTHER THINGS

"I'm a fervent fan of whatever William Gray writes, and though it was starkly different from his other works, this newest novella has only fed that fervor. A departure from the multi-faceted tales he's given us so far (but leveraging the same voice and tact), NORO is a bare-knuckle cage match with terror's true form. Gray mainlines the isolation, helplessness, and dread straight to your heart."

— Ben Young, author of STUCK and HOME

"Repulsively compulsive, Gray's novella will have your brain begging you to stop reading, while your heart keeps you going. Such a perfectly brutal read."

— Steve Stred, author of MASTODON and
CHURN THE SOIL

"William F. Gray's NORO is a chilling story about survival, guilt, and loss. The story follows two neighbors battling a horrific parasitic entity with vivid descriptions that will leave readers terrified."

— Jay Bower, author of CADAVEROUS and
THE TERROR OF WILLOW FALLS

"This lean and efficient snow-isolation nightmare is relentless in its drive, infection paranoia, and body horror."

— Andrew Najberg, author of GOLLITOK
and THE MOBIUS DOOR

Does the Dog Die?

For every kid who has ever had their life come apart and found peace within the pages of a scary story.

Chapter One

"It'll be a goddamn doozy, that's for sure," Con said, fiddling with his gloves. The cold was vicious, almost living, and it searched out any exposed skin to sink its teeth into. "You sure you don't want to holed up at my place?"

Jonah knew that was the best decision, or at least the safest one, but he shook his head. "Nah. Noro and I will be alright up at my place. We had it weatherproofed last year."

Before everything fell apart. Jonah didn't add on that last part, but it slunk from the recesses of his mind like a monster out of a movie. It always did when he least expected it; sometimes when he fully knew it would, too, like he'd summoned it with the power of thought. Trying to push the onslaught of emotion away, he focused instead on the truck before him. They only had one more chain to put on the front right tire of Con's old Toyota Tacoma.

"You got enough food? Firewood?"

"Yeah, I stocked up in town last week. The shed's full up, and I got a cord and then some." He'd been cutting firewood for the last five days, since the forecast had changed. It had been a long time since he'd seen as much snow as they were calling for, but he was at least prepared for it. Or as prepared as he could be.

"I just don't like you up here on your own," Con continued.

Jonah sighed, trying to keep his attention on the task at hand, but between the pain in his back and his frustration at Con's constant nagging, he was ready to explode.

Constance "Con" Jennings had lived out in the woods west of Jackson, Wyoming all his life. He was made for this life in a way that Jonah was not. His body, twenty years younger than Jonah's own, was lean and muscular from manual labor and hard winters like the one coming. His hair was greying, but only at the temples.

Jonah, on the other hand, was a large, burly man. He'd been in shape in his twenties, lost it in his thirties, and never found it again. His own body was soft, without sharp contours. When he looked in the mirror now, the only six-pack he saw was the Miller Lite on his nightstand he'd brought to bed with him.

Life can be hard in different ways, though.

As Con crouched down on the balls of his feet, Jonah fought the urge to push him over just to get him to shut up. They'd known each other for almost two decades, since right after he'd bought the cabin for hunting and summer vacation, but they'd only been friends in a passing way. 'Hi' there, 'hello' here. When Jonah showed up at his doorstep with a six-pack three months before, it was purely out of desperation for some sort of human connection.

In this moment, he regretted it. Sometimes Jonah viewed Con as a stray cat he fed once, and now couldn't get rid of. Nothing against the man himself—they were a generation apart, and Jonah was crabby to begin with. He just wanted to be left alone until he felt like some company, and he didn't want to be pestered about his safety.

That's not how relationships work, Jonah. The phantom voice of his wife. There was a malice behind the words that stung Jonah. She'd never spoken them, but his mind remembered her voice so well that the darkest thoughts sometimes hid behind her memory, turning it into a puppet.

"I'm just saying, *if* you change your mind..."

"I'll trudge through two feet of goddamn snow to get over here with Noro on my back if I need to," he said through gritted teeth.

Con, completely missing the rage boiling beneath Jonah's facade, grinned. "Hopefully you change your mind before it gets that bad. You know me and Doc would like the company."

Doc was Con's German Shepherd. The dog was young and beautiful, albeit a little hard headed. He remembered those days with Noro, before the arthritis started to get bad over the last year.

"Speaking of dogs," Jonah said, standing up and rubbing his cold hands together to try to get some warmth back into them. "I should be getting back to mine."

"I don't know how you can stand it out here without your gloves on," Con said as Jonah reached into his pocket and retrieved a pair. They were dense, wool glittens, with the flap to cover Jonah's exposed fingers for when they got cold.

"They get in the way of the chains, even with the fingers cut out of them. Makes harder work."

Con nodded. "Thanks again for doing it. The last few years, I just kind of let it ride and hoped for the best, you know?"

Back in 2019, Con had been working on a job site when a miter saw came off its track. A total freak accident. It had claimed the middle and pointer finger of his right hand, cutting them off at the first and second knuckle respectively. Now, he spent his time at home with Doc working on random projects while the disability checks rolled in.

Can't really hold a hammer too good anymore, he'd said to Jonah one drunken night. *At least, that's what I tell disability.*

While he might be milking it for the check most of the time, Jonah knew that it was a real obstacle for him other times. Like when he tried to put snow chains on his tires, for instance.

"No problem. If something happens, we'll both be glad they're on there."

"No kidding! If you want, we can go inside and grab a beer to relax and warm up, then I can..."

Jonah put up his hand, quieting Con. "I really appreciate it, but I really should get back to Noro. She's been in the cabin for a while now."

"Let me make it up to you later, then. Come on by for dinner. I've got a stew on, and it'll cut the cold right out of your bones. Plus, free beer."

As much as Jonah didn't want to, he knew that Con wouldn't take no for an answer. And if he just didn't show, the younger man was likely to traipse through the woods with a pot of boiling stew in hand.

Plus, free beer.

"Alright. Six sound good?"

"Sounds good. And bring Noro—I'll set a bowl out for her, too."

Chapter Two

There was about half a mile between Jonah's cabin and Con's, but the path was clear. At some point, both places had been owned by Con's father. The dirt at Jonah's feet was like concrete, the loose soil packed down by however many feet had traveled it all those years ago. It was almost like he was preserving their legacy by continuing to use it.

The cold wormed its way beneath the fibers of his clothes as he walked. Even with his thick, greying beard his face felt like it was frozen solid as he made his way through the naked trees.

A column of thin smoke rose in the sky—his cabin. The wood stove would still be burning strong when he got back, which was a good thing. It didn't take long for the temperature to drop once the fire was out.

When Jonah reached the small clearing the cabin was built on, usual pang of sadness reminded him of what he'd lost. The place was the basis of many good memories with his wife and sons, but now it was more like his punishment. He'd been banished here, something even he thought he deserved.

Everything had looked so different when he'd retired the year before. Now, it felt like the world had lost all its color, both metaphorically and literally. He was a sixty-seven year old man living alone in the middle of Bum Fuck, Wyoming, in the season when the winter steals the vibrancy of the state. Everything was shades of grey now, except for the few trees that stayed green year round, but even those seemed listless somehow.

I need to talk to Dr. Fields about an increase, Jonah thought as he reached the porch and climbed up to the door. The Lexapro did a good job of keeping his mood level, but sometimes the darkness was too much. It poured over, like a sink with the water left running, and all he could was stand there and watch when it happened.

Opening the door, he was greeted with a soft growl.

"Hey, girl."

Noro lay on a blanket by the stove, her ears perking up at the sound of his voice. She was a beautiful Blue Heeler, her coat almost entirely grey now with old age, but her eyes still held the keen intelligence that Jonah remembered when they picked her out of the litter ten years before.

When she saw Jonah, she clambered to her feet and made her way to him. She moved slowly and methodically. It was the calculated gait of a dog who knew pain.

"Bad today, huh?" He knelt down, feeling his knee pop with the action, and pet her between the ears as his eyes met hers. Noro's tongue hung from her mouth as she looked up at him, as if smiling. *Always the optimist.* "Let's get you some medicine."

After a few more scratches, Jonah climbed to his feet and made his way to the kitchen. It was an open floor plan, with only three rooms closed off from the main area: two bedrooms and a bathroom. Opening a cabinet door, he retrieved an amber vial with a prescription label on it. *Noro Henderson.*

Jonah popped the lid off and shook a generic looking white capsule into his palm. It was a Gabapentin capsule, but only fifty milligrams. He paid good money to a compounding pharmacy to have it made for her. It helped with the pain, but kept her alert at the same. The one hundreds made her sleep too much.

Next, he made his way to the fridge and retrieved a piece of American cheese. Wrapping the pill up in it, he held it out to Noro. "Here you go, girl."

Noro took it from his hand, gobbling it up like it was going to disappear any second.

As Noro finished her treat and medicine, Jonah made his way to the living room. A silver, blocky box that read SYLVANIA rested below an older television that he'd bought when the kids were still in middle school. For being a thirty year old TV, it worked pretty well.

A shelf was set up beside the entertainment console, and Jonah took his time perusing the titles there. At this point he knew exactly what was there and where it was, but there was something he liked about actually searching. It helped clear his mind, made him more excited to watch something.

He settled on the original Halloween film—a classic if there ever was one. Pulling the case from the shelf, he popped the disc from its place and clicked the small button beside the disc drive of the DVD player. The tray slowly appeared, as if it was struggling to perform this simple task it was designed for.

Jonah set the disc in the tray and nudged it. The small plastic piece disappeared back from whence it came, and he made his way to his favorite chair. Picking up the remote, he turned on the television and waited for the menu to come up.

By the time the movie ended, it would be just about time to make his way to Con's for dinner. Once he was done with that obligation, he'd return and descend into a hopefully dreamless sleep.

It was the best he could hope for.

Chapter Three

The stew was good, as he had expected. Con might be a pain in the ass to someone as grumpy as Jonah, but the man could cook.

"Want another beer, old timer?"

"Sure, why not?"

Jonah was a few beers away from sloppy drunk at this point, but he didn't care. Noro could lead him home without any trouble, and the path between their houses was completely flat with nothing directly along the side of it.

Meaning, no risk of being tripped. *Except over your own two feet, you drunk,* he scolded himself silently. In response, he tossed back what was left of his beer as Con returned with another glass bottle. The last sip was almost always entirely backwash, but he wasn't one to waste a good beer. Con bought the expensive stuff, so even when it was mixed with his saliva it was still tasty.

"You got enough gas out there for your gennie?" Con asked as he collapsed onto his old couch. Judging by the shape it was in, Jonah figured it was older than the man sitting on it.

"I've got enough gas to keep the generator running for a week straight. Can you just relax? Fuck me."

Con raised his hands in surrender. "Sorry, sorry. Somebody's got to worry about you, is all."

Because my family sure as hell doesn't. Jonah cracked open his beer and took a long draw from the bottle, as if toasting the thought.

"It's fine. I don't mean to be a bitter asshole."

"I get it. No harm, no foul."

Looking to change the subject, Jonah pointed at Doc. He sat by the wood stove with Noro on the other side of it. They looked almost like a mirror image of each other with their heads on their paws. Doc's eyes watched the two men while Noro slept peacefully.

"He looks good."

"He's good company. Good dog, too," Con said, taking a swig of his beer. Then his face darkened. "We're lucky to have found each other when we did."

"When I picked up Noro, my wife was *pissed,*" Jonah said, his speech slurring. "We'd been talking about getting a dog, and I passed this dinky little stand out on the road. When I stopped, there she was—in a goddamn apple crate with four other puppies. Something just told me to do it."

Con nodded. "What was the big deal? If you'd talked about it?"

Jonah's expression screwed up with frustration. "Heelers have a reputation of being nippy. Since both of our boys were married, Diane thought they wouldn't bring their future babies if we had a dog like her in the house."

"Ah. Sounds about right."

"Never had any problems, though," Jonah said warmly as he looked at his dog. "She's always been the perfect dog."

A heavy silence fell between the two of them. There was an open door there; an opportunity to broach a subject that Jonah both wanted to visit and avoid. He hadn't talked to anyone about it yet, and though he thought it might do him some good, it was the last thing he wanted to do.

"Want to watch a movie?" Con asked after the quiet had stretched on a little too long. "I've got some great comedies. I could seriously piss myself laughing at Meet the Fockers, man."

"Maybe next time." Jonah was almost *too* drunk now. "I'm gonna get back to mine, if that's okay."

"Oh. Okay." Con looked a little disappointed, but that was nothing new. Whenever Jonah took off, he always looked like a hurt little boy after his playmate had to go home.

"I'll see you sometime this week, alright?" Jonah assured him as he pulled on his coat. "After the snow melts a little and we can get down here."

"Sounds good, Jonah. You got your CB set up over there, right?"

"I do," he lied. The truth was that he'd gotten as far as mounting the tall antenna to his roof but never actually plugging it into the box. The wire was still curled up on the roof. "I'll chat with you on there tomorrow or something."

"Even if you don't, that's cool. I just wanted to make sure, cause once a storm like this hits..."

"Phones get a little wonky, you've told me. I'll see you later, Con."

He opened the cabin door and grimaced as the cold rushed in to meet him. Turning, Jonah whistled hard. Noro's eyes flew open, and she jumped to her feet and crossed the small cabin. *Gabapentin's still working*, he thought as Noro joined him on the porch. The difference in the dog was notable.

"See you, man!" Con called out as Jonah closed the door.

Now alone with the bitter Wyoming winter, Jonah and Noro began their trek home—man and best friend, both unsteady but together, as the snow began to fall.

Chapter Four

Jonah had been gone for maybe three hours when Con heard the crash.

The force of it shook the foundation of the cabin. Already feeling off balance from the alcohol, Con would have hit the floor if he hadn't been able to grab the counter in front him.

As soon as he heard it, Doc began to bark ferociously as he jumped to his feet.

"What the fuck was that?" Con asked himself, stumbling to the window and looking through the curtains there. The snow now coated every surface, maybe four inches deep already. It reflected what little moonlight seeped through the clouds, giving the night an ethereal appearance.

Squinting, Con spotted a warmer light off through the trees.

"Oh, *shit*."

Whatever had caused that sound, it appeared to be burning.

Feeling much more sober now, Con sprinted to the coatrack

by the door and began to throw on his winter gear. Doc was already there with him, ready to get out and find out what the source of all the commotion was.

Con opened the door as he pulled on his second boot, sweat pouring off of him. If there really was a fire, he had to get in the truck and get over to Jonah's as quickly as possible. It would spread quickly through the woods and reach the cabins in no time.

As soon as the door was cracked, Doc wormed his way through it and took off into the dark.

"*Doc!*"

There was no use. The German Shepherd either didn't hear him or didn't care. All Con could do was watch as he disappeared into the woods.

"*Shit, shit, shit,*" Con muttered as he ran into the kitchen and retrieved his flashlight. When he emerged out into the night, the first thing he noticed was just how cold it was. The temperature had dropped impossibly fast with the arrival of the storm. Casting his light at the large thermometer hanging from a tree at the edge of the porch, he saw it was just above zero.

"*Doc!*" Con yelled again, following the paw prints in the snow. He could still hear his barking from up ahead and the warm glow was diminishing by the second. *At least there's that.*

The wind gusted, cutting at the exposed skin of Con's face. His scraggly, red beard did little to keep his face warm as he chased after Doc. Every year was like this, but he didn't think he would ever get used to it.

The chug of the generator began to fade as he made his way deeper into the woods. As the sound grew quieter, his anxiety rose. Doc's barking suddenly cut out, punctuated by what was undeniably a pained yelp. Con froze, his heart hammering against his frozen chest.

"Doc!!!" He screamed, panic edging into his voice. *"Doc! Doc, where are you?!"*

Con began to jog, which quickly became a full out run as more cries from his pet filled the night. He called out Doc's name again and again as he sprinted through the darkness. The fire was almost out, but he could see that he was nearly there. Just a little farther...

Con's foot caught on a root hidden by the snow. His forward momentum caused him to stumble once, twice, three times, before finally falling. He hit the ground hard, feeling the air rush out of his lungs as the flashlight flew from his hand. The snow was so cold his hands burned like they were on fire as soon as they disappeared beneath the white powder.

Scrambling to his knees, he stopped at the sight before him. A large, five-foot round crater blocked his past. It was a black blemish on an otherwise pristinely white landscape. Small tendrils of smoke still rose from the edges of it, and what looked like a split rock rested in the middle of it.

Not a rock. Meteor.

A fucking meteor..

He was in awe of it until he looked past it. Then his stomach dropped and a single thought filled his mind.

Doc.

The contrast of the blood in the snow was almost as jarring as the crater. It started as a few drops, increasing in number and concentration before ending right where the German Shepherd lay in the snow.

"Doc, no!"

Con skirted the edge of the crater and slid to a stop next to his dog. The amount of blood on the ground seemed almost impossible, and he immediately felt helpless. *No, no, no...*

Doc whined, trying to lift his head and look at his master. "Stay still, boy."

He tried to figure out what to do next. The fear of hurting Doc worse if he tried to lift him crossed his mind, but he also knew there was no chance for survival if he left the German Shepherd out in the elements.

After a moment of deliberation, he slid his arms under the dog and lifted him up. The yelp that followed was like an axe splitting him down the middle, but he couldn't let it slow him down.

Taking off in a full sprint, Con rushed Doc back to the cabin as the smoking crater continued to cool in the falling snow.

Chapter Five

Jonah never heard the meteor. He didn't hear Noro barking, either. His consciousness was firmly occupied with the nightmare.

He threw open the door to the cabin and immediately knew what he was experiencing wasn't real. Wyoming had been transformed overnight, if it was. The winter was gone, the world had thawed, and now it was alive again. Vibrant.

Then he spotted the 1993 Ford Explorer in the tall grass, and dread crept in.

His legs carried him despite his mind protesting the action. The Explorer grew closer, and he found himself looking inside the open hood.

Ivy, wildflowers, and crabgrass had somehow worked its way through the engine, climbing through razor-thin crevices and coming out the other side. Jonah spotted a thick bed of moss covering the reservoir for the windshield wiper fluid; a layer of clover coated the valve cover.

Stopping at the fender, he leaned over and inspected the

unlikely blend of nature within the manmade machine. He wondered if this was what his old car looked like in whatever junkyard it had ended up in, but he would never know for sure.

He straightened and made his way around to the driver's side of the Explorer. The damage was just as he remembered it. Both doors were crumpled and caved in. The frame was twisted and bent from the force of the collision. The back window of the driver's side was shattered, but the driver's window was still mostly intact. An intricate spiderweb of cracks radiated from a bloody center.

Jonah?

Jonah spun on his heels, searching the clearing for some sign of the voice that he recognized. Despite the warm sun, he realized that he was freezing cold. He let out a breath and watched it mist out in front of him.

"Diane?"

The open door to the cabin moved ever so slightly. He tried to remember if he'd left it open or not when he'd stepped out, but couldn't. It didn't matter regardless. He was going up there no matter what the answer was.

Jonah made his way back to the porch, this time on his own accord. The phantom voice buzzed in his head as he climbed the steps and entered the small structure. The space inside the cabin was even colder than the outside. It was as if he'd stepped into an industrial freezer. Wrapping his arms around himself, he walked toward the center of the room.

A hiss, followed by a beep filled the air. He froze mid-step, terror creeping into his heart as a cold sweat broke out all over his body.

Hiss. Beep.

The master bedroom was located at the northeast end of the cabin, the other bedroom at the northwest. The crack under the door to bedroom that his son's had shared was dark, but a sterile, white light illuminated the other.

Hiss. Beep.

Don't do it, Jonah. Don't do this to yourself.

Knowing it wasn't in his control, Jonah approached the door to the master bedroom without urgency. There was no doubt about what he would find behind that seemingly innocuous door he'd opened and shut a million times in the real world.

He reached for the handle and turned it...

Chapter Six

Jonah awoke with a start, sweat pouring off of him despite the chilly bedroom. His eyes darted from left to right as his waking mind tried to rectify the sterile white room he'd just witnessed with the reality of his dark bedroom.

"Jesus…" He finally said, hanging his head and holding it in his hands. At his feet, Noro whined and looked at him with concern. "I'm okay, girl."

It was a lie, but it felt like a good one. *Necessary,* for both him and his only companion. After another minute to let the adrenaline ease out of his system, he threw his legs over the side of the bed and made his way across the cold floor toward the door.

He hesitated with his hand inches from the knob, remembering his dream. It recurred every night, never beginning the same but always ending with that day from his memory. It haunted him in a way far more real than ghosts or demons ever could.

Pushing through the feeling, he opened the door and made

his way across the main room to the stove. The embers there glowed an angry red but gave off little heat. He cursed at himself for being so stupid. It was one thing to drink yourself stupid, but he'd been so drunk he'd forgotten to put any wood into the stove. He'd almost let it go out.

Jonah opened the metal door and reached to his right, retrieving two pieces of wood and throwing them in one after the other. Next, he grabbed the bellows and began to blow air at the embers. They flared up, turning a brighter red, then orange.

Within a minute, both pieces had caught. Sitting back, he watched as the small fires spread and became larger before joining together. There was something relaxing about it. He'd always liked fire since he was a kid. It was as mystical as it was practical.

The *click clack* of Noro's nails joined the crackles from the stove. He didn't turn as Noro joined him at his side. The Blue Heeler sat down and leaned against him. Wrapping his arm around her, he felt her soft fur in his hands.

It was comforting, that familiar feeling. Things seemed so uncertain for him, but he could always rely on Noro.

Together, the two watched as the fire grew to a roar within the confines of the stove.

Chapter Seven

"*Doc! Doc, stay with me!*"

The kitchen table was covered with blood. It dripped from one corner, forming a puddle around the leg.

Con searched frantically for any sign of physical trauma to the dog, but he couldn't find it. His hands were sticky with Doc's blood. They came away crimson no matter where he touched the German Shepherd.

Doc's breathing was becoming more inconsistent by the minute. One second, the dog's breath came in fast, shallow bursts that made Con afraid he was dying right then. The next, Doc would take deep, hitching breaths that made his body convulse.

His fingers reached for the dog's belly, and came away bloody yet again. It was like Doc was sweating blood.

Suddenly, the Shepherd yelped as if it had been hurt. He tried to jump to his feet but the table was too slick. Doc's legs slid out from under him, and he returned back to his previous position on his side with Con's gentle urging.

"It's okay, boy. It's okay. I'm here... I'm..."

A loud crack filled the cabin and something moved beneath Con's hand. He cried out as Doc yelped again, but didn't try to move this time. His tongue lolled out from his open mouth as he panted.

Con's heartbeat sped up as another crack resounded through the small space. He watched with horror as Doc's ribs —previously barely visible beneath the small layer of fat around his midsection—jutted out impossibly far. The two closest to his stomach were disfigured, as if they'd been...

He was watching when the third rib snapped under the internal pressure it was experiencing.

"What the *fuck?*"

Doc's whines were growing in volume, causing Con to circle around to look at him. The German Shepherd's eyes were glazed over, and his saliva was a sickly pink color from the blood in his mouth.

"Oh, Doc..."

Whatever was happening, it was killing his dog. His best friend. Shit, his *only* friend, if you didn't count Jonah.

He went to Doc, reaching out for him. Doc's tag wagged ever so slightly at Con's touch, who was now openly crying. He gently pet the dog, leaning forward so his eyes were within inches of Doc's.

"I'm so, so sorry, buddy. I don't know what happened... I don't know how to help..."

But he did. Doc was suffering in a way that he could never have imagined. He had to do something to make it stop.

"I'll be right back, Doc. It's almost over."

Con ran to his desk in the corner of the cabin and threw open the drawer there. It was mostly filled with loose papers, batteries, paperclips, and all sorts of other junk a single man might collect over the years—but it was the Glock there that he was interested in.

Pulling the gun from the drawer, he slid the slide back and chambered a round reluctantly. He was sick with anxiety and guilt over what had happened, what was happening, and what was about to happen.

Behind him, another rib cracked. Doc yelped, reassuring Con that he was making the right decision.

He turned and slowly made his way to Doc. The anxiety was joined by sadness as he looked down at his dog. "God, I... I... I'm so, so sorry, buddy."

Con gently reached out with his free hand and scratched Doc between the ears, just how he liked it. The German Shepherd's eyes cleared for a moment and met his, and his tail wagged once.

A wheeze escaped Doc's throat, and his entire body went limp.

"Oh, Doc..."

Part of him was relieved that he hadn't had to put Doc out of his misery, but Con felt immense guilt for having prolonged it as long as he had. He should have gone for the pistol the moment he got back with the dog, but he'd been panicked. His desperation to save Doc was stronger than anything else he'd been feeling.

Turning the safety back on, Con walked back to the desk and placed the gun on top of the desk. A bottle of whiskey, almost entirely gone, rested on top of the scattered stationary there. He grabbed it, screwed off the top, and took a swig.

Crack.

Con spun, his eyes wide as his throat burned from the cheap whiskey, and looked toward Doc's body.

The cabin was eerily quiet except for the ambient sounds

of the fire in the wood stove. He took a tentative step toward the dog, his heart returning to its rushed rhythm from before.

"Doc?"

There was no movement in response. His companion's muscles remained limp as he approached. There was no question that he'd heard the sound, but it didn't make any sense.

Just the fire popping.

That was wishful thinking, and poorly orchestrated at that. He knew what he'd heard. The crack had been identical to that of the breaking ribs he'd heard before.

And what was with that, anyway? The whole thing made such little sense.

Con reached Doc and laid a tentative hand on his bloated stomach. He hadn't realized it before, but the dog's abdomen had ballooned to almost twice its normal size. He almost looked pregnant.

A choked sob escaped from his throat. The German Shepherd was already losing heat, his bloodied skin becoming cool to the touch. Con grabbed a handful of Doc's coat and gripped it, pulling at it softly.

"Oh, Doc..."

Something long and thick shifted beneath Con's hand. Beneath Doc's *skin*. Con cried out and stumbled backward, tripping over his own feet. He hit the ground hard, flying backward and slamming his head against the hardwood floor.

"Ah, fuck..." He grumbled. The pain in his head was severe, and he was more than a little dizzy as he sat up. Looking toward the table, he gasped.

A tubelike shape wove its way through Doc's broken ribs, working its way up to the back of his neck. Con's mouth hung open as he scrambled backward. All he wanted was to look away, but he couldn't stop watching.

The shape reached Doc's skull and stopped moving.

26

The silence was only punctuated by the fire in the stove and the wind outside. Con's head throbbed as he tried to make sense of what he'd just experienced.

Then Doc's back left leg moved. It was a jerky motion, one that seemed almost involuntary. It grew still again for several long seconds before moving again, this time slowly. Deliberately.

"What the…"

Now Doc's front legs joined the one already moving, starting out with the same spasmodic motions and becoming more fluid with each moment. The back right was the last one to join.

The cabin grew still for a moment, and then Doc's head rose from the kitchen table. All Con could see were the whites of his eyes as Doc turned toward the him. The German Shepherd's jaw was slack, moving from side to side. His tongue lolled out, trying to move but succeeding in only squirming.

It was almost as if Doc was relearning how to control his body.

No. Not relearning. And not *Doc.*

The meteor. The snake-like shape moving through the Shepherd's body, breaking ribs. The way it stopped right at the base of the skull, where it could…

Doc's mouth snapped shut, but his tongue was still hanging there. Sadness and fear mixed with anxiety as Con watched a chunk of the dog's tongue fall to the floor. Fresh blood poured from his muzzle as he—*the thing controlling him*—learned how to growl.

"Oh, *fuck.*"

Con turned and scrambled toward the desk. Toward the gun.

The sounds of growling and hurried nails on the hardwood followed him.

Chapter Eight

A gunshot ripped through the night, tearing Jonah from his doze beside the stove. Noro leapt to her feet, barking instantly as her master climbed to his feet and ran to the window.

The snow was falling harder than before. There had to be a solid six inches out there now, turning the world into a negative image of the one he'd fallen asleep to.

A second gunshot echoed through the woods. Jonah wasn't an expert by any means, but he'd fired enough guns to know that it wasn't a rifle like the Winchester 94 he had by his door.

Con.

A deep sense of dread sunk into his gut as he thought about the younger man. He knew that Con had a pistol, and the gunshot sounded just like the Glock Jonah had heard fired before when the other man had used it for target practice. There was little doubt in his mind that something bad was happening just through the trees.

"Goddamnit."

Noro was still barking, but Jonah didn't scold her. He was just as spooked as she was, so it wouldn't be fair to chastise her.

The first thought he had was to try his phone, but he knew it would be useless. Grabbing his Samsung, he touched the screen just to confirm that he had no reception. From what Con had told him, that was pretty typical during a winter storm like this one. Which was why he'd given Jonah the CB radio in the event of an emergency.

The CB radio he'd neglected to hook up.

Pulling on his winter gear in a hurry, Jonah tried to think about his options, which there was really only one.

"I'll be right back," Jonah said as he slipped into his boots and tied them. The Blue Heeler whined as he stood up and opened the door. The cold rushed in like a living thing searching for refuge. A strong desire to just stay inside arose within him. Let it be.

Let it be—like you let it be before?

The voice of his younger self, one who hadn't been alone and ridden with a guilt that he couldn't escape, cut deep.

It also spurred him into action.

Grabbing the Winchester 94, he pulled back the bolt and verified there was a .30-30 cartridge there. The familiar shimmer of gold brought him more anxiety than it did peace of mind, but he would be thankful for its presence if he needed it.

He turned back to look at Noro, who stood in the center of the cabin. Her bright eyes were sharp, begging to come with him, but the rest of her betrayed a lack of youth. The snow was coming down hard and he couldn't risk her getting hurt.

She was all he had left.

"Be a good girl," Jonah said, closing the cabin door behind him and stepping into the white oblivion of the woods.

The first thing he noticed as he left the shelter of the porch was how windy it was. He'd felt it coming through the door, but out in the open it was a tempest trying to push him back toward the woods. There was no thought of turning back now, though. As much as he claimed to dislike Con, he was the closest thing Jonah had to a friend.

And he needed help.

Jonah found the going slow, but he pushed on. His feet were heavy like they were encased in concrete. Each step took immense effort. The snow was easily seven inches now in the clearing, but the wind had formed snow banks in the woods where it had collected against clusters of trees. From where he was, he figured he saw at least one spot where the snow was a foot deep along the path.

"Fuck me," he muttered. Deciding that having his hands for stability was more important than the comfort of the rifle in them, he slung the strap over his shoulder and hurried into the woods.

The cold bit at him though his bundled clothes. He pulled down the flaps of glittens, covering his previously exposed fingers, and tried not to agonize over what awaited him through the woods. The two gunshots had been followed by total silence, a fact that meant one of two things.

Either Con had taken care of the problem, or it had taken care of him.

What little light that seeped through the dense clouds reflected off the snow and lit up the woods, but Jonah still found his visibility limited by the swirling flakes of the storm. He could see ten feet in front of him, maybe fifteen when the wind died down, and he imagined all sorts of horrors hiding just beyond his line of sight. The most mundane of them was wolves—the worst, impossible monsters.

Con, you better not be drunk and just shooting off your fucking gun.

It was a possibility that he hadn't thought of before, but he found it unlikely. He'd been out at the cabin for over six months and Con had never drunkenly fired his gun late at night.

But if he was wrong, it was a costly assumption. Jonah imagined his head exploding as Con fired on the strange shape materializing out of the storm. *Turn back. This doesn't concern you. You can just...*

Jonah growled to quiet the voice of reason in his head. Maybe it was right, but he couldn't just turn his back on Con. Couldn't *let it be...*

A sudden vision, jarring in its clarity and vivid realism, hit him. He saw Diane climbing into the old Explorer, the Virginia sun reflecting off the dark green paint job that didn't have a single scratch on it. It had been unbelievably hot that day, and he'd been in the yard cutting the grass. He'd let it go too long, just like he'd let the fuel injector go too long...

A warm yellow light began to develop through the haze. Jonah froze, instantly afraid as he imagined an angel materializing before him to pass judgement for his sins.

It took him a second to realize what he was actually looking at.

The lights from Con's cabin.

He'd been so lost in thought he'd somehow lost ten minutes of time. It seemed almost impossible, but then again, the cold had a way of making one disassociate to cope with it. One foot after the other; don't think about your appendages turning blue.

Picking up the pace, Jonah broke through the tree line into the front yard of Con's cabin. The bank of snow here was so deep that he had to push the top of it out of his way. The snow was now a solid nine inches deep, coming halfway up his calf, and he knew he had to hurry up. If he waited too long, he'd be snowed in with Con, and Noro would be left alone.

"Con!" Jonah called out, his voice hoarse from the cold. "It's Jonah!"

There was no answer.

Pulling the flaps off of his exposed fingers, he cupped them around his bearded mouth. "I heard gunshots! Is everything okay?!"

Still, silence.

A deep unease settled into the pit of his stomach. "I'm coming up!" Then, muttered to himself, "Don't... shoot me."

Jonah made his way across the snow covered yard and up the steps, feeling unbelievably exposed as he did so. He'd been lucky to never have to fight in any of the wars some of his peers had experienced, but he imagined camouflaged enemies with rifles all the same.

Or just one drunk man with a pistol.

He reached the door and knocked twice, hard. "Con? You in there?"

More quiet greeted him, and then...

"Jonah..."

It was whispered, as if wrestled from the depths of Con's chest with the last of his strength. If it hadn't been so goddamn silent on the other side of the door, Jonah would have missed it entirely.

Panic gripping him, Jonah grabbed the knob and turned, only to find it locked.

"Con? Con! Open the door!"

No response.

"Con, goddamnit! Con!"

After only another moment's hesitation, Jonah stepped back and kicked the door as hard as he could. It shook in its frame, but didn't budge. He was still a big man, even in his old age, but he'd undeniably lost some of his strength with the passing years. Thirty years ago the wood would have buckled around his boot.

It only took two more hits before the frame broke with a

resounding snap, swinging inward and letting Jonah see the inside.

"Jesus fucking Christ."

He'd grown up religious, something that hadn't stuck, but some things still were engrained in him like old ghosts that wouldn't let go. One of them was taking the Lord's name in vain—*goddamnit* was okay, but something about *Jesus Christ* always made him feel dirty.

He could count the times he'd uttered those words on one hand, and this was the only time he'd slipped a *fucking* in between them.

The amount of blood inside the small cabin was deeply alarming. Clustered drips led the way from the front door to the kitchen table like paint dribbles, but then it looked like someone had knocked over an entire can of crimson paint. It coated every inch of the surface of the table, leaking over the sides and forming small puddles around it.

"*Con?!*"

A single thump from somewhere out of sight. Jonah pulled the rifle off of his shoulder and turned the safety off. The cold behind him seemed like a warm comfort as he stepped inside the cabin.

The scent of rotten meat hit him hard enough to double him over. Gagging, Jonah fought the urge to vomit. The air was thick with the stench.

"*Jo-n-ah,*" a voice croaked from somewhere just out of sight. *The island*, Jonah thought, looking toward the square block situated to the left of the kitchen table. The voice was just on the other side of it. He unzipped his jacket and reached into the inside pocket of it, retrieving a handkerchief. It was a striking blue in comparison to the muted colors of both the cabin and his own attire. Slinging the rifle back over his shoulder, he realized how entirely out of place the piece of cloth looked as he placed it over his mouth and tied it off behind his head. It did little to stifle the smell, but it was better than nothing.

He pulled the rifle off of his shoulder again and slowly made his way toward the island, careful to sidestep the blood on the floor. There was so much of it that it seemed like a nearly impossible task, but he managed to avoid it for the most part. When he was directly between the kitchen table and island, he noticed the boot and paw prints scattered along the floor randomly. It almost looked like art, if it weren't for the horrible connotation of what must have transpired to create them.

Jonah rounded the corner, bringing the rifle up...

Only to lower it when he spotted Con.

The man was in bad shape. His jacket was torn on the left arm and covered in blood, the white cotton puffed out of the ripped fabric a deep red. His leg was soaked, and Jonah spotted a belt wrapped around it. *Make-shift tourniquet.*

"Con... Holy Hell, man..."

Con let out a choked sound. "Hurts..."

"What happened?!" Jonah set the rifle on the ground and knelt next to the man. His knee landed in puddle of fresh blood, but all concerns of avoiding it were forgotten. The overalls he was wearing were waterproof, anyway. "Where's Doc?"

As if in response, the door to the bedroom shook with violent force. A snarl, distinctly canine but somehow off, reverberated through the cabin.

"In there," Con grimaced, trying to adjust himself. Jonah saw a nasty bite mark where his collar met his neck and swallowed hard.

"Doc did this?"

"Not... Doc..."

The German Shepherd slammed into the door again with a

deafening crash, then began to dig at the wood with his paws. "What do you mean, *not Doc?*"

"Doc's dead, Jonah."

Con's voice was cold and detached, making Jonah suddenly feel like someone had dumped a bucket of ice water over him. "Dead? What? How?"

Con shook his head, then pointed to the sink. Immediately understanding, Jonah climbed to his feet and grabbed a cup. First he tried to fill it with water from the tap, only for the pipes to creak and grumble angrily. *Frozen.* He began to throw open cabinets until he found what he was looking for. It only took a second to pour a cup of water from the recycled milk jug, and then he was back at Con's side.

The man drank greedily, and as soon as he took the cup from his lips, Jonah thought he looked a little better. When he spoke, he certainly sounded more like himself. "Something came out of the meteor, Jonah."

"*Meteor?*"

Con's face contorted with confusion. "You didn't hear it?"

"No, I came when I heard the gunshots..."

The man's expression changed again, this time hardening as he grabbed Jonah's forearm. "It doesn't matter. Something came out of it, man. It fucking got Doc. Got *into* him."

"You aren't making any sense..."

"Most of this blood is his. He was like... *sweating* it, Jonah. Sweating *blood.*"

Con was clearly delirious from blood loss. Whatever had happened to him—and to Doc—had clearly been horrific, but wires were being crossed in his brain because his body didn't have enough blood to carry oxygen to it. Meteors? Sweating blood? None of it made sense. Maybe a wolf attacked Doc, and then Con. That would explain the gunshots.

"Listen, we've got to get you to a doctor..."

Con's grip tightened on Jonah's arm, hard enough to make him gasp. "*Jonah,* you aren't listening."

"You're hurting me..."

His grip didn't ease. "His stomach was bloated. He looked almost pregnant. He died, Jonah. I watched him die."

There were tears in his eyes, and Jonah couldn't help but feel sympathy for the man. He imagined what he would feel like if a wolf had gotten ahold of Noro and had to fight the urge to hug Con.

"I'm so sorry, Con..."

"Then something moved inside him." The way he spoke the words sent a shiver down Jonah's spine. "It broke his ribs, man. It worked its way up to his spine—his *brain*—and then stopped. Then *he* moved. His legs... they started moving. It was like he was relearning how to use them. His jaw, too."

Despite how absolutely insane Con's words were, he couldn't help but feel fear's stone-cold grip on his nervous system as Doc crashed against the door again. He looked toward it and wondered what the hell was really going on.

"I shot him, Jonah."

His heart froze like a cog stuck. Turning back, he found Con looking at him with a dazed, confused expression.

"What?"

"I shot him. *Twice.* Once in the fucking *head.* And he didn't die. *Because he's already dead, Jonah. He's already dead.*"

Con began to cackle, his laugh that of the clearly insane. When the door splintered behind him, Jonah fell backward and turned toward the sound. Doc's head jutted from a jagged, uneven hole about the size of a plate.

What was left of Doc's head, anyway.

"Holy *shit!*"

CHADBOURNE

Con's laughter died as he reached down beside him. Jonah wasn't sure how he hadn't seen the pistol laying at the man's side, but his jaw slacked with surprise as Con raised it. The sound of the gun discharging made Jonah jump as it went off. The round missed Doc's head, piecing the wood just below the hole.

The bullet did the job, though. Doc disappeared back into the dark recesses of the bedroom, retreating for the moment.

"How..."

"It'll only slow that thing down for a minute. It's how I managed to drag him back there... but I wasn't fast enough." Con gestured to his bloody leg. "We gotta get out of here, man."

"The CB..."

"Already tried it. Either no one is listening, or the storm knocked over the antenna."

"Con..."

"We gotta get back to your place," Con muttered, gesturing with his head. "That door won't hold, and you've got bars on your windows, right?"

"To keep rowdy teenagers out, not fucking zombie dogs..."

"We've got to go *now*. Before it gets out."

"We'll shoot it again..."

"*No*." Con's voice was stern and loud, not at all like the one he'd been using since Jonah found him on the floor. "If it gets out and suddenly bullets *don't* slow it down, what are we going to do?"

The prospect of that—and the fact that it was definitely possible—made Jonah feel like pissing his pants. That was also a real possibility, considering how bad his bladder was getting with his old age.

Looking at Con, he tried to think if they even had a chance to get back to his place. Con was badly injured, and the snow would undoubtedly be nearly a foot deep now. They would be moving slow, and if Doc *did* get out and give chase, there was no way they could outrun him.

Or it.

You could always leave Con. That'll slow Doc down.

The thought, intrusive and horrifying, made him angry. Then something else occurred to him.

"Where are the truck keys?"

Con pointed to a hook by the door.

"Come on," Jonah said, pulling Con to his feet. The man grimaced with pain as Jonah pulled him to his feet. Next, he slung the Winchester 94 over his left shoulder and pulled Con's arm around his shoulders to help support him. He motioned for Con to hand him the pistol after a moment.

At first, he thought Con was going to refuse. Then the man begrudgingly placed the Glock in Jonah's free hand.

Shoving it deep in his pocket, he half-helped, half-dragged Con to the door. After retrieving the keys, the two men stepped out into the raging snow storm.

Chapter Nine

Con remembered the day he brought Doc home.

It was a hot, summer day. The sun was shining bright and he was on his way back from the grocery store. Bags shifted in the bed of his truck as he shifted into second gear and pulled out of Jackson. It was a short drive down the main drag before he had to turn off, and it was right before here that he saw the black tote in the middle of the road.

"*Fuck!*"

Con slammed on the brakes, fighting the urge to cut the wheel as well. He knew how that ended from his experience—he'd flipped the first truck he'd owned on this very road at nineteen. *Lucky to walk away with your life*, the deputy had told him. *Many don't.*

The black tote was all he could see as the tires squealed against the pavement. At the very last minute, he let off the pedal and turned the wheel ever so slightly, missing the plastic box by mere inches. Slamming back down on it, he came to a full stop about ten feet away on the shoulder of the road.

If anyone had asked him why he'd stopped, he would have

told them intuition. As ridiculous as that sounded, it was the truth. There wasn't a specific reason he could give to why he climbed out of his idling truck and approached the tote. There were no thoughts of hidden treasure or the like. Something just told him to do it.

He reached out and grabbed the handle, pulling it toward the side of the road. A muffled yelp came from inside and his stomach dropped.

Pulling the lid off, he'd braced himself for the sight he knew would be waiting for him.

Out of the litter of six German Shepherd mutts, there was only one survivor. Tbe puppy, barely four weeks old, shook with fear when Con pulled him out of the tote and hugged him close to his chest. The temperature inside the plastic sauna must have been well over one hundred degrees. The tiny dog's tongue hung from the side of his mouth, and Con felt a moment of pure panic.

He was too late to save the poor thing.

The puppy needed water, and fast. Con cradled the poor dog as he sprinted to the truck. There were four jugs of fresh spring water there—a luxury he usually didn't spend on, but the well-pump had been acting up lately. He'd only bought them out absolute necessity. The one single time he'd ever had to do it.

He yanked the tailgate down and set the poor puppy down on it. Next, he grabbed one of the jugs and pulled a knife out of his pocket. Water splashed on the tailgate, his jeans, and his shoes as he cut the top three-quarters off of the jug and gently pulled it to the puppy.

Con saw that the puppy's eyes were glassy, and he felt that fear again. No creature should have to die like this. Especially not one as young as this one.

Cupping his hand, he dipped it into the cut jug and gently

poured it into the puppy's open, panting mouth. Most of it splashed on his muzzle or the tailgate, but it did the trick. A glint of sharp recognition replaced the unseeing sheen over his eyes, and he raised his small head toward the jug.

The small dog tried to stand, but was too weak. Con slipped his hands underneath his belly and helped him up, and watched hopefully as he drank greedily.

"Woah, little fella. Not too fast..."

After he was sure the puppy had gotten enough, he placed the little German Shepherd inside the cab of the truck and went to retrieve the tote. It was surprisingly light as he lifted it into the bed of his truck and slammed the tailgate closed.

Anger, so rare for him, burned bright as he climbed back into the driver's seat and drove the rest of the way home. The puppy, still weak, curled up next to him. When his hand wasn't on the stick shift, it was on the small form beside him.

When he pulled up to his cabin, he carried the puppy inside and set him down on the faded dog bed beside the stove. Instantly, he began to sniff every inch of the ratty old thing, taking in the strange scent of another dog. Buzz had been gone for six months now, but Con guessed dogs could smell those things for a long time after they'd become invisible to the human nose.

He grabbed a couple slices of cheese and ham, put them on a paper plate, and sat it in front of the bed. The puppy didn't waste any time bounding toward the food. Con wondered when the last time he'd eaten was and experienced another flash of rage.

As the puppy ate, Con retrieved the bags with the cold groceries in them and placed them on the counter before stepping back outside. He made his way to the small shed at the corner of his property and retrieved a shovel before returning to the truck.

So light, Con thought again as he carried the tote into the woods. It didn't take him long to dig the hole—in fact, it took him longer to put the small forms inside of it.

Con wasn't a religious man, but he said a prayer for each one as he placed them inside the hole anyway. They'd deserved better than what they'd been given, and he hoped that they were in a better place than the one they'd left.

Later that night, Con gave the small puppy the name Doc. It just came to him, and it felt right after all the wrong he'd experienced that day.

Doc.

Doc.

Doc...

* * *

"Doc..."

Con was whispering the dog's name again and again, barely audible over the roaring wind at their backs. The snow was over a foot deep now, and dragging Con through it seemed impossible. Every muscle on Jonah's body strained and screamed in protest with each passing step.

"Come on, man, you've got to move your feet..." Jonah growled as he reached out for the door handle of the Toyota Tacoma. It was so snow covered that it looked like a mountain buried under the powder substance. Searching blindly with cold fingers, he finally located the handle and yanked the door open. Snow cascaded from the door and off the roof, piling up at their knees.

"Doc... I'm so sorry..."

Jonah wondered if it might already be too late for Con. The path they'd cut through the snow was dotted with the man's blood. Longer red smears marked where Con's injured leg had dragged across the surface.

Easing the other man into the cab of the truck, Jonah watched as Con's eyes sharpened with recognition.

"Jonah..."

"I've got you. Let's get you out of here."

Jonah slammed the door before Con could say anything else. The snow surrounding the truck was far too deep for Jonah to run around the front like he wanted to. It took a solid thirty seconds to reach the driver's door and climb inside the cold truck.

"The snow, Jonah... it's too deep..."

"We've got the chains on the tires. It'll be fine."

Jonah slipped the key into the ignition and turned it. Listening to the engine crank brought his anxiety to a whole new level as he imagined the truck refusing to start.

"Jonah..."

The engine roared to life. It was almost deafening in the void created by the snow storm.

"Alright, let's..." Jonah's voice died as he looked out the windshield and saw nothing but pure white. "*Fuck!*"

Climbing back out of the truck, trying his best to ignore Con's cries, Jonah went to work clearing the truck off. His face and fingers stung from the cold. The thick wool fabric of the glittens was soaked as he tried desperately to hurry. He used his arm as a shovel, pushing off the mountains of snow in long, sweeping motions.

"That'll have to do," Jonah said, leaving the cold behind and slamming the door. "Let's get out of here."

"Will you please listen to me...?" Con's voice was low, weak from blood loss, but angry.

Jonah put the truck in reverse and looked over his shoulder. "Easy does it..."

He eased on the accelerator, felt the tires catch for a moment, only for them to start spinning the next. Easing off the pedal, he repeated the cycle one, two, three, four times. On the fifth, he spat out a curse.

"There's not enough weight, Jonah."

He spun on Con. "What?"

"That's what I've been... trying to fucking tell you. The bed is empty. I didn't think... to load it with anything."

The bed is empty. Without some sort of substantial weight in the bed of the truck, the tires would just keep spinning. All that would accomplish would be packing the snow down tight, making a hard, slick surface that even the chains would have trouble gripping.

Jonah swallowed hard. "You've got the firewood stacked on the porch, right? If I hurry..."

"You don't have enough time. You gotta get back to the cabin, try your radio..."

His face burned hot as he looked at Con. "I never finished hooking it up."

"Are you fucking with me? Why the *fuck* wouldn't you just set it up?!"

"I never even asked for it," Jonah snarled. "You forced it on me because you think I'm some feeble old man..."

"You *are* some feeble old man!" Con shouted, his voice breaking and hoarse. "I'm sorry, Jonah, but you're sixty-seven years old. This place... it isn't your friend. You've only ever been out here in the summer. You have no idea what it's capable of."

Jonah opened his mouth to fire back, but closed it slowly. As much as he hated to admit it, Con did have some valid points. At the very least, he definitely hadn't expected the storm to turn this fast, and he sure as hell had never imagined he'd be dealing with...

With what? A zombified dog? Some extra-terrestrial parasite?

As the silence stretched on, some of Con's resolve melted away. "Listen, man..."

"I'm going to try to make it back to my cabin and get the CB working."

"In this storm?!" Con voice dripped with shock. "You'll get blown off your roof..."

Jonah's mind was already working. Con had fueled up before the storm, meaning he could easily last twenty four hours in the warmth of the truck before running out of gas. Probably longer. It would buy Jonah enough time to get help.

Assuming he even made it back to the cabin before Doc got out.

"The antenna is already mounted. I just need to run the cable. I can just run it through the window, make the call..."

"There's more than just the elements to worry about."

"I know. But this is our only chance."

Con chewed on his lip for a minute, then gave one curt nod.

"Okay. Okay." Jonah pulled the pistol out of his pocket and went to hand it back to Con before pausing. He imagined the man turning it on himself if the truck died and his stomach lurched threateningly. *You can't just leave him out here without something defend himself with.*

Deciding he didn't have much of a choice, he pushed the Glock into Con's hand. "I'm going to grab you a couple jugs of water and something to eat, okay?"

"There's jerky in the pantry."

Nodding, Jonah climbed out of the truck, but Con grabbed his forearm. The look on the other man's face gave Jonah's pause when saw it.

Con carefully pushed the rifle on the seat between them

toward Jonah. "Put another round in him—*it*. To slow it down again."

The prospect of what Con was saying made Jonah feel queasy. "Okay..."

With that, Con released his grip on Jonah's arm. After grabbing the rifle, Jonah slammed the door of the truck as the cold wind whipped around him. His joints creaked as he trudged through the snow toward the open cabin door. The anxiety he was experiencing only grew as he neared the warm glow spilling out onto the porch.

No matter how hard he tried he couldn't wrap his head around what he'd seen. Thinking about the blood on the floor, he had to struggle not to vomit. There was no way that Doc was still standing, especially after being injured the way he had seen, but Jonah had seen it with his own two eyes.

His hands hurt from holding the rifle so tightly. He adjusted his grip and pressed the stock to his shoulder as he entered Con's cabin again, listening for the mangled dog. His eyes found the door and locked onto it as he quietly made his way to the kitchen. He retrieved two jugs of water from the still open cabinet before shooting a glance at the pantry door. It was around the corner from the bedroom—meaning that he wouldn't be able to keep an eye on it while he looked for the jerky.

Just get it over with. The sooner you get out of here, the better.

Jonah hurried over to the pantry, being careful to avoid the blood on the floor. He slung the rifle over his right shoulder as he went, instantly feeling exposed without it. *Just don't think about it.* The door opened with a creak, sending his adrenaline into overdrive. A quick peek around the corner revealed no movement in the ragged hole Doc had put into the door.

"Okay, okay," he whispered to himself, "You've got this."

He was trying to relieve some of his anxiety, but it seemed hopeless. His stress levels were through the roof, and it didn't feel like it was going to abate anytime soon.

"Come on, come on."

When he found the jerky, he let out a long sigh of relief. Turning, he made his way across the kitchen to the water jugs. He picked them up and went to leave, when something on the floor caught his eye.

Little white shapes moved throughout the puddle of blood under one corner of the table. Their movements were slow and lazy, but enough to draw his attention. He knelt down at the edge of blood in an attempt to get a closer look.

They looked like little white centipedes. Their bodies were too slender to be maggots but too white to be some sort of worm, and the jagged legs that jutted from their sides gave them a dangerous appearance.

Where did they come from?

Before he could formulate a solution, a low growl cut through the sound of the wind whipping through the front door. Jonah bolted upright, his attention moving straight to the bedroom door. A pair of eyes reflected the light from the rest of the cabin, twin orbs staring out of the darkness beyond the hole, soulless and full of ill intent.

His hands shook as he backed away toward the front door. He almost dropped the bottles and jerky and went for the rifle, but he couldn't bring himself to do it. No matter what Doc had become, Jonah couldn't separate it from his memory of the German Shepherd.

Con's words echoed through his mind. *Put another round in him. It.*

Jonah turned and fled the cabin as another growl trailed behind him. Back out in the cold winter elements, he began to realize just how perilous things were becoming. The snow was falling impossibly fast now, and was almost up to his knees in places.

Gotta get back.

"*Con!*" Jonah screamed, but his voice was stolen by the wind. Coughing, he made his way back to the driver's side and opened the door. The next thing he saw was the muzzle flash of Con's gun.

Chapter Ten

The fever was unlike anything Con had experienced. His entire body shook despite the heat now blowing from the vents of the truck. Sweat, sticky and sweet, clung to every inch of him and soaked his undergarments.

What the fuck is happening to me?

The nausea was the worst part. It was like being seasick, but a hundred times worse. Even the slightest movement of the truck made him feel like he was going to hurl.

He'd first started to feel sick shortly before Jonah arrived. *Chalk it up to blood loss,* he'd thought. Now, he wasn't so sure. He remembered the fake illness in Stephen King's *The Stand* and thought that was exactly how he felt. The gun in his hand was freezing cold as he watched Jonah disappear into the cabin through the windshield, the wipers working double time to keep the glass clear of snow.

As soon as his friend stepped foot into the cabin, Con had a horrible thought.

This is the last time I'll ever see him.

The image of Doc, half of his skull missing, tearing into the tender meat of Jonah's neck was like a power drill burning a hole through his mind. The bit struck oil in the form of a new level of fear, excavating an indescribable terror from deep within his psyche. It was the sort of thing a child feels when left alone in a dark place: indescribable, total, infinite.

"Jonah," Con croaked, and realized how badly he needed a drink of water.

The only response he received was a low, continue growl. Whipping his head around, Con searched for the source. It was an unrelenting, surrounding him like a pack of wolves.

Doc got out. Doc is out here, and he's coming for me. Coming to finish the job.

Con raised a shaking hand and wiped sweat from his eyes. Looking down at his hand, he saw that it came away blood red. A small squeak escaped him as he squeezed his eyes shut.

Oh God, oh God...

A piercing bark—or maybe a breaking branch—scared him badly. He jumped and immediately regretted it as bile rose in his throat. It took everything he had to push it back down. His eyes darted from place to place, imagining shadows moving against the backdrop of the snow storm. A quick glance back at his hand revealed that it was slick with sweat, but not blood.

Before he could think, the growling picked up in intensity. The entire truck groaned, as if it too were afraid of the monster outside.

Con flicked the raised the gun, swinging it from left to right as panic dictated his every move. His imagination, aided by fever, ran wild. Any moment, Doc would materialize out of the falling snow and crash through the window, all gnashing teeth and bloody flesh.

Movement caught his eye, and he watched a shadowy figure appear at the door. His finger tightened on the trigger as the dome light came on and he fired. The sound was deafening in the small space. A shrill ringing overrode every sound in the world.

At least I can't hear the growling...

It wasn't Doc, Con realized with budding horror. Wind flooded in through the open door, a deafening roar that his brain had misunderstood for that of the monster his companion had become.

And dogs don't open doors.

"Jonah...?"

Chapter Eleven

Blood leaked out from under Jonah's hat and down his cheek as he rolled to his side, pressing a hand against the left side of his head. The wound burned, like someone had heated a knife and tried to scalp him. Black dots hovered behind his eyelids from the muzzle flash and a low whine underscored the sounds of the blizzard.

"Jonah...?"

Jonah sat up and backed away, pulling the rifle from his shoulder and raising it in one fluid motion. His finger stopped just short of the trigger as Con dropped the gun and raised his hands.

"What the fuck were you..."

His voice trailed off as he looked at Con and took in the sight before him. The man was plastered with sweat, his skin almost as pale as the snow Jonah now stood in. Dark circles stood out under his eyes, which had taken a listless sheen.

Lowering his rifle, he rushed to the truck.

"Jonah, I'm so fucking sorry," Con croaked, but Jonah didn't bother listening. Pulling his hand out of his glove, he pressed the back of it to Con's forehead. Jonah was freezing, but he could immediately tell that Con's fever was out of control.

The water. Jonah rested the rifle on the floorboard of the truck and turned around, searching for the jug. It was already almost covered with snow, only identifiable by the red cap that every company that made whole-milk used. He pulled it out of the powder and began to for the jerky, but it was gone.

"Jonah..."

"I'm looking for the jerky, hold on..."

"I'm not hungry, man."

Jonah cast a glance over his shoulder and stopped. The expression on Con's face was equal parts misery and terror. It was a look that he had never seen before, but now he imagined his wife would be wearing it in his nightmares from now on.

"What?"

"I just... need the water, please."

Jonah obliged, thrusting it at the man as he tried to think about what to do. With the current rate of snowfall, he was running out of time to get back to the cabin and try to set up the radio. It would already be a nearly impossible task, and he didn't even really know what he was doing. If he fucked something up, it was likely that Con was going to die right here.

If you leave him in that truck, he's dead already.

Somehow, Jonah knew that was true, too. His condition was seemingly getting worse by the second, and he badly needed a fever reducer and antibiotics, at the very least.

Whatever he's got, I don't think antibiotics will fix it.

As Con drank greedily, Jonah slung the rifle back over his shoulder and picked up the pistol. The blood on his face had already frozen, leaving the left side of it feeling stiff.

"Con, we've got to go."

His friend stopped drinking. "What?"

"I've got medicine back at my house. Clindamycin, for dental procedures. It's not much, but it's something. It'll hold you over until help can get here."

"Jonah, I can't make it that far."

"I'll drag you if I have to. If you stay here, you'll die."

"If I go with you, *you* could die."

Jonah stared at Con, who shrank from the expression on his face. "You're coming with me, Con. You aren't dying out here alone."

The wind gusted, and snow blew in through the open truck door. Con opened his mouth to argue, reconsidered, and instead reached over and turned the key in the ignition. Pulling the key out, he let his lanyard drop to the floor.

"Okay. Let's go."

Jonah wasn't sure if he was relieved or more anxious by Con's choice. He knew that they were both right about what was going to happen next. Either Con would die from exposure or sickness, or the both them would die at the teeth of his demon-dog. His thoughts turned to Noro and swallowed hard.

It's not an option.

Pushing away his dark thoughts, Jonah stepped to the truck and helped Con climb out into the now knee deep snow. He immediately began to shake, and Jonah slung an arm around him to help him stand. Con draped his right arm around Jonah's shoulders and looked at him, his eyes cold and emotionless.

"If it comes, you have to leave me. Promise me."

"Okay. I promise," Jonah lied after only a moment of hesitation.

Interlude

The world was such a strange place.
Cold, dark, and wet.
The sensations the meat felt were so odd. The stickiness of the blood, the cold that clung to the ground with such relentless intensity, the taste and smell of smoke that gently hung on every particle of air.
Not that it needed to breathe. It simply did that to keep the heart pumping; only kept the heart pumping to keep the circulation up. Cold was universal, not exclusive to this place. If blood stopped pumping, then its limbs would atrophy. It was inevitable, anyway. The parasite could only manipulate so much. Each time the meat's heart spasmed, pushing blood in and out of it, yielded a diminishing return.
The cells were dying.
It needed to find a new host before then. This one had not been capable of surviving the process, and once all life function truly ceased within it, the parasite could not survive for long in the temperate conditions of this place.
Forcing the host to lick its lips, it approached the hole it had created. The barrier between this space and the larger, more open one was already weak. Light—beautiful, blinding—flooded in through that small gap between here and there. It felt the pupil of the meat's one remaining eye dilate in response to nearing it.
It needed to find the other one, before it was too late and this host died.
The name, enunciated in such an unfamiliar tongue, was ever-present...

Joe-nuh.

Chapter Twelve

Within minutes, Jonah decided that it was more than likely that both he and Con would die out in the storm. The wind was relentless, slowing the progress as much as the snow itself. He couldn't see more than a few feet in front of him; the path was nonexistent.

It didn't help that he was more or less dragging Con through knee high snow. The man had no strength left in him, and Jonah had to stop more than once to let Con vomit. Whatever was wrong with him, it had come on fast and it was progressing faster.

Gotta get him out of this storm.

The two men trudged on, Jonah guiding Con toward what he hoped was safety.

Distance was immeasurable. Everything was a sheet of white, with dark pillars materializing out from behind the lacy veil of the falling snow. The wind blew steadily, the gusts enough to almost knock them over, and the snow froze in Jonah's beard. He imagined he looked similar to Jack Nicholson by the end of *the Shining* by now.

"Jonah..."

Con's voice was weak and shaking. His whole body trembled against Jonah's as they fought against the elements. Each step took everything that Jonah had. His muscles ached from the exertion.

"Jonah, something's wrong."

Jonah cast a glance toward his friend and saw Con holding his midsection. His face was pained as he looked up at Jonah, but there was fear beneath his expression.

"I think..."

Con pushed away from Jonah and leaned against the nearest tree, vomiting uncontrollably. The sound made Jonah feel queasy, but he slowly approached Con anyway. His instincts were screaming at him that something was off, that something was really, terribly off in a way he'd yet to realize...

Wiping his mouth of, Con looked at Jonah with serious eyes. "I think Doc's coming, Jonah."

"You can't know that."

"I'm telling you, you've got to leave..."

Before Con could even finish his sentence, Jonah grabbed him by the collar and yanked him back in the direction they'd been heading.

"Shut the fuck up and *move, then!*"

Con pushed back, somehow remaining standing despite his sudden illness. The act looked like it took everything out of the man.

"Get your fucking hands off me!"

The two stood several feet from one another, Con's expression partly obscured by the falling snow. Jonah's entire body shook with each breath as he looked at his neighbor.

Things were well out of his control. The storm was raging, dumping snow on them at a rate he couldn't believe. They were likely lost, heading in the wrong direction, and would never reach the cabin.

Would never reach Noro.

"We have to keep moving," Jonah said, his anger bringing heat back to his frozen cheeks. "If we don't get to the cabin, we're going to fucking die out here."

"I'm telling you, it's coming. If you don't leave me, you're as good as dead."

"I'm not leaving you, you stubborn fucking asshole. So let's get..."

Jonah's voice died in his throat as Con pulled the pistol out of his jacket pocket. His hand immediately went to his own pocket, only to find it empty.

Con had stolen it.

"I'm not fucking asking."

"Con..."

Raising the gun, Con fired a single round into the air. The sound dissipated too fast, the echo carried away on the roaring wind.

"You've got to go."

Jonah almost listened. It was the easy way out, the one where he was most likely to survive with his beloved pet. Even if he did get back to the cabin with Con, the man was clearly sick. What if it was contagious?

Then he thought about Diane. What would his wife have done, if she had been here?

As he looked at his neighbor, his only friend who he had treated with such disdain so many times, he felt ashamed.

"Con, you're going to have shoot me."

The gun shook in Con's hands as the two men stared at each other. There was a long, horrifying moment where Jonah thought he might actually pull the trigger. He'd forgotten that Con had already tried to shoot him once, albeit in a fever induced panic. Next time, Jonah might not be so lucky to escape with a simple graze.

"Fuck," Con muttered, lowering the gun. "You're a stubborn old son..."

* * *

"...of a bitch, you know that?!"

Jonah stumbled backward, still in shock, as his son pushed him as hard as he could. Alex's face was contorted with rage and grief, turning him into a stranger in the sterile white light of the hospital hallway.

"I didn't... I... I..."

"How many times? How many times did I tell you that you needed to get that fucking death trap fixed? Replaced? How many fucking times, Dad?!"

Jonah felt small. His entire being screamed in agony as he looked around, trying to make sense of what was happening. When he'd gotten the call, he had laughed. Actually laughed.

There was no way something like this could happen to them.

Alex stepped forward, closing the distance between the two of them. "She's gone because you. If you had just listened, and gotten the goddamn fuel pump fixed..."

The rage Jonah experienced in that moment, looking into his youngest son's face, scared him. It was foreign, yet familiar. He grabbed Alex by the shirt and pushed him backward until he hit the wall hard enough to crack the drywall. The sound of the plaster caving in snapped him out of it as quickly as it had come. When he looked down at the hands holding onto his son, they weren't his own.

They were his father's.

He forced his fists to unclench. The action was painful; his grip on the fabric of Alex's polo had been impossibly tight. Taking a step back, he looked in the eyes of his son and knew.

He'd lost more than his wife today.

"I'm sorry..."

"Tell that to Mom."

As silence fell in the hall, the only sounds came from the room they stood outside of.

Beep. Hiss. Beep. Hiss.

Chapter Thirteen

"Jonah, you okay?"

Jonah snapped back to the present. Suddenly, he was staring at Con through the sheet of snow instead of his son under the harsh fluorescents of the hospital.

"Yeah, I'm... I'm fine." His ears rang with the two sounds that would haunt him for the rest of his life. *Beep. Hiss.* "We've got to get moving."

As Jonah neared, he froze in shock. The sweat pouring off Con had frozen solid, encasing his face in a thin sheet of ice that cracked with each facial expression. *He's going to die of hypothermia if I don't get him somewhere warm.*

A howl cut through the wind. It was impossible to tell how far away it was, but Jonah could immediately tell that it sounded wrong. It warbled and cracked, like the animal it had escaped was learning how to do it for the first time.

"Jonah..." Con said, his eyes wide.

Before he could say anything else, Jonah ripped the gun from his hand grabbed Con around the waist. The man jerked away from him, but Jonah was considerably stronger than him at the moment. Forcing Con's arm around his shoulders, he began to move through the snow faster than he thought possible.

The one thing that they had working for them was the fact that Doc also had to negotiate the hazardous conditions. Con might be dead weight, but he imagined that the German Shepherd would have great difficulty getting through what would soon be two and a half feet of snow...

Jonah stopped and turned, his eyes falling on the narrow trench his legs had made. It was still mostly filled with snow, but it would a hell of a lot easier for Doc to navigate than he had originally thought.

He only let himself dwell on it for a moment. Returning his attention forward, he picked up his previous pace. His legs, back, and Con screamed in protest.

"You gotta fucking leave me, Jonah!"

Jonah ignored him despite how loud Con's voice was in his ear. The gun in his hand was ice cold against his uncovered finger tips but he didn't dare put it in his pocket. The last thing he wanted to do was give Con an opportunity to lift it off him again.

The wind was a constant whoosh that drowned out everything but their labored breathing and Con's curses. It took everything he had not to turn back every few seconds to see if the dark form of Doc was chasing them, coming out of the white like a developing photograph.

Keep going. Just keep going.

Up ahead, the trees began to thin and Jonah's heart leapt as he realized what it meant. He pushed forward, barely keeping hold of Con, and hit the snowbank at the edge of the clearing his cabin sat on. It was nearly four feet high where the falling snow had piled up against the tree line.

"Con, hold onto the tree!" Jonah screamed, letting go of his

neighbor. He shoved the pistol in his pocket and began to dig as fast as he could, throwing handfuls of snow behind him as he tried to clear the path enough to drag Con through.

The roar of the wind heightened his anxiety. It hid all the other sounds of the world, masking any approaching threat. He let himself turn now, and the absence of any shapes appearing out of the storm did little to ease his mind. After Jonah had finally cleared enough to get Con the rest of the way, he reached out his friend and pulled him toward him.

The two men broke through the tree line, stepping out into the open. The cabin was a thin silhouette set against the snow storm, growing dark and gaining more detail with every step.

"Come on, come on," Jonah whispered, his entire body on fire.

"Jonah!"

Con's arm left his shoulders and shoved hard, pushing the two of them apart. Both men went sprawling as a black shape flew through the air where they'd been standing. Blood tripped on the white snow as it came crashing down, disappearing beneath the white. Jonah rolled away, pulling the rifle off of his shoulder as snow fell down over him.

He heard the growl and had just enough time to raise the rifle with both hands. The Shepherd pounced, landing on top of him. Doc's neck pressed down against the rifle as his teeth gnashed and clacked in Jonah's face. His hands and arms screamed with the exertion. The barrel was freezing through the glitten of his left hand, the stock slick against the one on his right.

Fuck, fuck, fuck, I'm losing it...

Jonah stared up into the half-destroyed face of Con's dog and did the only thing he could think of. He slammed his head forward into Doc's muzzle and heard a deafening crack.

Fear gripped him a moment too late—*what if the sickness is in his blood?*—but it was unwarranted. The Shepherd's muzzle bent at an ugly, impossible angle, but there was no blood.

For the first time, Jonah noticed the stiffness of its movements. Doc's body was impossibly firm, and he realized that it was frozen solid.

Suddenly, Doc stopped biting and began to choke. It was the sound dogs make when they've eaten something that doesn't agree with them, like grass, and are about regurgitate it on your floor.

A scream erupted from Jonah's throat and he threw his head to the side as he tried to push his attacker away. Doc refused to quit, though. The Shepherd's entire weight was baring down on the rifle Jonah was using to hold the dog at bay.

This wasn't grass.

From inside, loud, piercing barks cut through the wind.

Doc's remaining ear perked up and he stopped trying to expel whatever it was in his throat, and Jonah took his chance. Summoning strength he thought he'd lost, he surged forward and threw the Shepherd backward. As he watched the dark form of the dog disappear into the snow, he scrambled to his feet and sprinted for his door.

His feet found the familiar steps of his cabin and he barreled ahead, hitting the door and turning the knob in one motion. Snow swirled in around him as he slammed the heavy door shut with a crash, leaning against it. His left hand still gripped the rifle, the joints aching with cold and the beginning stages of arthritis.

Letting out a shaky breath, his eyes fell on Noro by the fire. The Heeler was on her feet, growling. Her eyes were brighter than he had seen them in years.

"It's okay girl, we're..."

His words died in his throat.

We.

He ran to the window and looked out into the curtain of falling snow, looking for any sign of the man that he'd left behind.

His neighbor. His friend.

"Con!" Jonah yelled out, his eyes frantically darting from side to side.

All he saw was white.

Chapter Fourteen

The cold was more intense than anything Con had ever felt. When he opened his eyes, all he saw was white. Panic took hold of him as he sucked in a terrified breath. His hands stung so badly inside his gloves that he couldn't close them. It took everything he had to roll over and push himself to a kneeling position. His wounded leg pounded as he searched the blizzard for any sign of Jonah.

A figure moved just at the edge of his vision, making his heart leap in his chest.

"Jonah?"

The shadow moved out of sight, fading into the white out. If it had even been there in the first place.

He crawled forward, his frozen face screaming in protest as he called out his friend's name again. When he only greeted by the whistling wind and the distant sound of cracking ice, he pulled his injured leg beneath him and tried to take a step. The pain he experienced was worse than he could have imagined, but he pushed on after the figure he'd seen.

A dark shape materialized out of the blizzard—Jonah's cabin.

He'd gone maybe a dozen steps when he saw it again, this time climbing the steps toward the door.

A small cry escaped his throat as his eyes fell on Doc's ruined corpse. Ice crystals covered most of Doc's fur, forming little icicles that jangled as it walked. The missing side of the Shepherd's head was coated in ice and snow tinted red.

Ice broke with each labored step that it took. The sound he'd heard over the wind was Doc moving through the snow even as the dog's corpse froze solid.

Its remaining ear twitched, and it turned to face Con. They were only five feet apart now. The storm had hidden Doc so well that he'd been virtually on top of the dog before realizing.

"Doc..." Con croaked. "Doc... please..."

He didn't know why he was begging for his life from this thing before him, but he didn't see any way out of his current predicament without some form of mercy from it.

It took a tentative step toward him, its unseeing eye searching his face. Con found himself reaching into his pocket in search of the pistol, even though he knew it was long gone.

"Doc, if you're in there somewhere..."

The corpse of his dead dog snarled, but it didn't sound right. It was like a poor imitation of the real thing.

The point got across, though. Con understood that he was about to die.

Taking a step back, he weighed his options. Doc was clearly faster than him in his current state, as proven by the distance the reanimated dog covered to catch up to them. If he tried to run, he would be dead before he got to the woods. He could try for the mountain of snow that was Jonah's car, but there was no guarantee it would be unlocked. Even if it was, Doc would be on him before he could clear the path to pull the door open.

All he had left was to stand his ground or let it take him. He decided on the former; his last act would be to try and rip the goddamn thing out of Doc and free him of this horrible fate.

Con balled his hands into fists and put all of his weight on his good leg, ready to strike. His body thrummed with anxiety as he watched Doc prepare to lunge, its frozen muscles cracking like branches under foot. The dog's remaining milky white eye remained locked on Con as it pounced.

The speed with which the dead German Shepherd moved caught Con off guard. He barely had time to get his hands up and grab the scruff of the dog's neck before it was on top of him. Inside, Noro began to bark wildly as he fell backward and landed on the ground hard enough to knock the wind out of him. His entire world went dark as he disappeared into the snow with the corpse of his dog at his throat.

The snapping of Doc's jaws sounded impossibly close to his face as he tried to push it away. It took everything he had to hold onto the frozen dog's neck—each time the Shepherd bit at him, it inched out of his grasp.

The parasite. Get the fucking parasite.

He wouldn't, though. Con wasn't sure he had the strength to just yank it out through Doc's frozen skin at his best, and he was far from that now. He was weak with pain, cold, and blood loss, and his resolve had faded the moment he'd hit the ground.

"*Con!*" Jonah's voice, rising above the roaring wind and gnashing teeth. "*Con, lift him up!*"

For a moment, he didn't understand what his neighbor was asking. Once he did, he was so exhausted still almost didn't even try. It was better just to let it happen. Doc's body convulsed in his grip and the Shepherd's jaw opened wider as it went for the kill.

It began to gag as Con's grip tightened on its throat, his fingers desperate for some form of purchase.

Whether he accepted it or not, it felt like the end.

Chapter Fifteen

All Jonah could see were thrashing shapes in the snow. His visibility was so limited that he could discern dog from man as he aimed the rifle at the chaos before him. Behind him, Noro barked and scratched at the closed door in a ferocious attempt to get outside to protect her master.

"Con!" Jonah called again. His entire body shook with terror as he watched the two going at it. It took everything he had not to pull the trigger despite not knowing who—or what— he was aiming at. If he shot Con, he wasn't sure that he could live with himself.

Or that he would, considering that Doc would then turn on him.

He deeply considered heading back into the cabin and locking the door behind him. Con was probably already dead anyway, and he had Noro to think about.

Maybe he would have before Diane, but now he couldn't. He knew that it would eat away at what little was left of him if he left Con to die.

"Con, goddamnit, listen to me!"

The wind was deafening, and if Con tried to reply at all, Jonah didn't hear it. All he could do was wait and see—

One of the shapes rose above the snow, and Jonah spotted a single pointed ear through the blizzard.

The report of the gun sounded like a cannon going off in the woods. The round caught the Shepherd in the back, throwing it forward and away from Con. Jonah didn't waste any time. As soon as the dog disappeared into the snow, he sprinted down the stairs and dived toward Con. His hands found his neighbor's jacket and yanked him upright. The momentum of the motion carried both of them to the stairs, and Jonah pulled him the rest of the way to the door.

"Noro, back!" Jonah screamed as he threw the door open.

The Heeler obeyed immediately, retreating toward the stove with a whine. As soon as he'd pulled Con fully into the safety of the cabin, he slammed the door shut. It wasn't a moment too soon.

As he slid the deadbolt into place, Doc slammed against the door with enough force to make the frame buckle. The sounds coming from the German Shepherd were feral and horrifying. It was what he imagined a rabid dog might sound like, but a hundred times worse.

"J-J-Jonah?"

Con's teeth chattered as he sat up and looked at Jonah. Outside, Doc roared with anger before colliding with the door again. There was no doubt in his mind now—Jonah felt the door shiver in its frame again.

The wind howled outside as Jonah tried to figure out what to do next. The storm showed no signs of abating—in fact, it looked like it was only getting worse. It was supposed to continue through the night and into the early hours of the following morning, meaning they could end up with well over three feet of snow by the end of it.

Leaving his place at the door, he crossed the short distance between himself and Con. "I'm so sorry, I didn't mean to..."

Con shook his head. "D-don't. Thanks for... c-coming back for m-me."

"Here, let's get you warm."

Jonah reached down and attempted to help Con stand, but the scream of pain that erupted from him was deafening.

"My... fucking... l-leg."

Doc slammed into the door again. There was no telling if the loud crack that Jonah heard was the wood breaking or the dog's bones snapping. Regardless, there wasn't another moment to waste. He made his way around Con and looped his arms under the man's arms. Jonah's back cried out in protest as he dragged his neighbor to the wood stove and set him down on the floor in front of it.

Adrenaline's fading, he realized. Every muscle in Jonah's body was impossibly sore as rushed to the couch in front of the TV. Planting his feet, he grabbed the arm and began to push. The feet squealed against the wood floor as he moved it across the space and placed it in front of the door.

"There," he panted. It might not be much, but he hoped it would be enough. Doc had been frozen solid when they'd struggled outside, which gave Jonah hope. If they could wait long enough, the cold would do what a bullet obviously couldn't.

His biggest concern now was Con. He would have to stop the bleeding in the man's leg if both of them hoped to see the sun rise the next day.

Jonah made his way to the kitchen, his mind racing as he tried to remember what first aid he knew. There was a kit somewhere under the sink, more of an antique than anything, but it had bandages, gauze, and even needle and thread. The truth was he had serious doubts of his ability to suture the bite marks, but it was a fact he would never reveal to Con.

The cabinet door screamed in protest as he threw it open. The darkness there was so thick it was almost alive, like an endless maw waiting to swallow him. It wasn't until then that he realized the lights weren't on. Standing up, he flipped the switch next to the sink.

Nothing followed the soft click. He jiggled it up and down, his chest tightening with terror as he realized the truth.

Sometime between when he'd left Con's cabin and now, the power had gone out. It had been an expected thing—it was why he'd stocked up on gasoline for the generator.

The generator that was located in the shed attached to the cabin, almost a dozen paces from the back door.

"Fuck..."

Jonah stood there for a moment, rooted in place, as he tried to think of his options. Things had just become infinitely more complicated. Without the generator, there were no lights or running water. There was a chance the pipes would freeze anyway, but he'd only bought enough water for himself and Noro for three or four days. Now, he had Con to worry about.

The realization of the problem led to yet another: *the firewood.*

Most of his firewood was stacked inside of the shed, away from the elements. He only had only brought eight or nine pieces inside the day before.

All but three were gone, and the stove was already nearing empty. They had only had enough firewood until dawn, and that was if they were lucky.

Would Doc be gone by then? Jonah certainly hoped so, but he couldn't say for sure. There was little doubt that the German Shepherd couldn't continue in the conditions, but he had to be careful. If he made his move too fast, the dog would be waiting.

Returning to the sink, Jonah rummaged around in the darkness for the first aid kit. The first thing he pulled out was an old flashlight. Flicking the switch on and off, he saw that the light was fairly dim. *Bad batteries.* Instead of using it, he stuck it in his pocket and went back to his search. When he finally found the kit, he made his way back to Con. The man had stripped his jacket off and was laying as close to the stove as he could get, sweat pouring off of him.

"Hey Con, how are you hanging in there?"

It was a stupid thing to say, but Jonah didn't know what else to say as he knelt down and opened the kit. The wrappers of the band-aids were yellowed with age and brittle to the touch as he reached in and began to pull out the supplies.

"My fucking leg is on fire," he said flatly.

After emptying the contents of the first aid kit, Jonah reached out and pulled open the stove. The fire there was indeed dying, but it gave an enough light for him to see more details.

Con's face was almost porcelain white, the only color there being the purple bags under his bloodshot eyes. His blonde hair was plastered to his forehead with sweat, so wet it was almost black.

"Jesus..."

"Jonah, something's wrong..."

Yeah, you're bleeding to death.

"I'm going to take a look at it, okay?"

Con simply nodded. A sudden, horrifying thought hit Jonah: *he's going into shock.*

He realized that Doc and Con were on two sides of the same scale, anxiously waiting each other out. It was a game of chicken to see who would break first, and as Jonah tore open the leg of Con's snow suit and then his thermal beneath, he realized he might be on the losing side of it.

The bite looked putrid, like it was already rotting despite having only occurred hours before. The skin was a dark purple and wrinkled like it had been submerged underwater for a long time. The dark punctures where Doc had latched on were black, bleeding holes.

I never should have left this cabin, Jonah realized as he collapsed back onto his ass. Guilt, ever-present because of his late-wife, had pushed him into action, and now he realized it was likely for nothing.

Just do what you can.

Suturing it would do no good, so he settled on grabbing a roll of gauze. He noticed how badly his hands were shaking as he unrolled it. The small amount seemed almost useless as he began to wind it around Con's injured leg. The white material instantly began to blot dark red as he made pass after pass. When Jonah reached the end of the roll, he reached out and grabbed the paper tape dispenser. The first inch of the tape had no adhesive, but after pulling it out of the spool further he found it passable.

Just one more oversight in a long history of them.

He should have bought a new first aid kit when he moved up here, if not a long time ago. This pitiful assortment of supplies that had likely been manufactured in the early 2000's was another painful reminder of his carelessness.

"How's that?" Jonah asked as he finished.

"Fine," the man groaned. "What are we going to do, Jonah?"

"Wait out that thing, I guess."

There was a moment of hesitation as Con hesitated. When he spoke, his words were low and remorseful.

"I don't think I have that much time."

Chapter Sixteen

The funeral was a quiet affair, reserved only for Diane's closest friends and family, and Jonah remembered every moment of it.

He spent the entire time standing among a small copse of trees near the edge of the cemetery, sweating in his dark suit. The heat had been sweltering that day, and even the shade provided by the leaves did little to provide refuge from it.

He couldn't hear what the pastor was saying. It didn't matter anyway; church had been Diane's thing, not his. This was about her, the children they shared, the friends they filled their lives with. Not him, though. There was no peace that any man or woman could offer him.

After a while, the service concluded. He only knew because the change in the body language of the attendees. Grief gave way to anxious impatience as they stood up and started to make their way through the headstones that blocked their path to the small one lane road that ran through the cemetery. They wove in between the stone monoliths, giving each one as wide a berth as they could, like to touch one would bring death upon themselves.

Jonah's eyes hovered between the fresh grave they were leaving and his two sons. Alex, his wife Roberta, and their daughter Erin made their way to the red Hyundai Tucson near the front of the line, while Keith walked alone toward his older Chevy Impala. Jonah had been surprised that Keith's son Kevin hadn't come, but co-parenting was a difficult thing and Keith had never been very good at showing up in his opinion.

Not that Jonah had any room to talk. His sin was much worse than Keith's.

After the last of the stragglers had reached their cars and drove off, Jonah trudged down the short hill from the trees he'd been hiding within and made his way to Diane's grave. The tombstone there was simple and tasteful, just like she would have wanted. As he neared it, he saw the carefully engraved inscription there.

Diane Miller
August 7th 1958—June 13th 2023
Beloved Mother and Wife

Jonah came to a halt at the side of the hole and looked down at the lid of the smooth casket there. His heart ached in a way that was far more spiritual than physical. He wanted nothing more than to climb down there and join his wife.

You did this, he thought to himself. It had become his mantra over the last week, and he knew that it was right. Maybe he hadn't killed her himself, but his inaction certainly had caused her demise.

"Hey, uh, buddy?"

Jonah turned, surprised by the unexpected visitor. A man in a dirty t-shirt, jeans, and an Atlanta Braves baseball cap stood there. When Jonah didn't respond and simply looked blankly at the stranger, the man shifted uncomfortably from foot to foot.

"Not trying to rush you or anything, but they've got the backhoe coming up here soon. Take all the time you need—just saw you standin' here and I didn't want you to be caught off guard."

Jonah simply nodded, flabbergasted by what the man had said. The idea that his wife would be buried and truly gone from this world in a few short minutes was too much for his mind to comprehend.

"Okay. Thank you," he said flatly. It was all he could manage.

The man excused himself and walked away, casting nervous glances back at Jonah as he went. After the worker was about a dozen yards away, Jonah returned his attention to the grave.

Beloved Mother and Wife.

He wondered what his would say, and he imagined it would likely be blank and only contain his name and those all-important dates. His sons would give him a tombstone, but they wouldn't have anything nice to say.

Jonah remained there until the thrum of the backhoe motor filled the still, humid air, then made his way to his parked car without looking back.

* * *

Stepping into the room where his boys had slept was a surreal experience that brought back that same ache he'd felt since Diane had passed. Her death—and his part in it—had created a rift between him and his sons that he worried would never be patched over.

His screaming muscles protested what he was about to do, but he didn't have much choice. He was feeding the stove with one piece of wood at a time, trying to make it last, but doing so wouldn't keep the entire cabin warm. The thought had occurred to him that he could break apart the furniture and use that if he needed to, but he also didn't want to inhale the toxic fumes of stain and varnish. The thought of Noro breathing in that poison was enough to make him feel ill.

No, he'd hold off as long as he could before doing that.

Jonah made his way to the bunk beds there and grabbed the bottom mattress. It took every ounce of strength he had to yank it from its place and drag it out into the living room, but he managed. Once it was in place beside the stove, he helped Con roll over on top of it. Next, he grabbed a pillow and blanket from the bedroom and returned. Shaking the dust off of both of them, he carefully covered Con up and placed the pillow beneath the man's head.

After making sure that Con was comfortable, Jonah retreated to one of the kitchen chairs and dropped onto it with a groan. Noro immediately joined him, laying her greying muzzle on his knee. Her fur was soft beneath his wrinkled hands as he scratched behind her ear.

The screaming wind outside made Jonah feel uneasy. He imagined Doc limping around out there in the cold, barely held together by frozen tissue.

How long would they have to wait until the elements finally put a stop to the undead German Shepherd? He didn't know—but he knew that every second was precious. Casting a glance at Con, he wondered just how long the man had left.

There was a hole in the foundation.

It found it because of the heat it could feel coming from the hole when it passed.

Digging with frozen paws that cracked but no longer bled, it cleared enough of the snow away to reveal grate set against crumbling concrete. A couple of hard hits knocked it loose, giving the German Shepherd entry.

Crawling on its stomach, it made its way under the cabin.

Cobwebs from the low ceiling clung to its matted fur as it wormed its way deeper. The dirt underneath was cold and hard, but the air itself was much warmer. Well above freezing, in fact. As it neared the middle of the space, it came to a stop. It was at its warmest here, the heat so intense in comparison to its frozen body that it burned.

It settled in, allowing the heat to do its job.

Then it waited.

Chapter Seventeen

Con awoke some time later, sweat plastering his clothes to him. The wave of nausea that washed over him was so intense it blinded him as he sat up. The cabin was impossibly dark, like all the light had drained out of the world.

Where the hell am I?

He racked his brain as he tried to remember what had happened. His leg hurt like hell, and his face stung like he'd been out in the cold for too long. And why was his bed on the floor?

Searching the darkness, he couldn't make out anything out other than the vague outlines of furniture. The wind outside sounded absolutely ferocious, threatening to knock down the walls that kept it out. He turned from side to side, fighting the urge to vomit, and spotted the dim light of a fire through the grate of a wood stove. It looked like it was almost out.

The click of sharp nails on the wood floor made the hair on the back of his neck stand up.

It's just Doc, there's nothing to be a—

The events of the night came racing back like a flash flood of images, overwhelming him.

The crash out in the woods.

Blood in the snow.

A meteor in a smoking crater.

Doc, sweating blood.

His ribs cracking as something worked its way through him.

The sharp teeth biting into Con's leg.

Con firing and taking half of the German Shepherd's head.

Locking Doc away, and Jonah's eventual arrival.

Their trek through the frozen wood as the snow deepened to above their knees.

Doc pouncing at him from the porch—

Sweat dripped down the side of Con's face as he reached blindly for something to use to defend himself. The sounds were getting closer now, and he imagined the half-destroyed head of his companion materializing out of the shadows.

It's Doc. He's coming for you, a voice that vaguely resembled his own whispered in his head. The fever was so intense that he almost felt drunk as his hand reached for something to grab hold onto.

Finally, his finger's closed on something just beside him. One side was rounded and the others ended in sharp corners— *a log.*

Con pulled it slowly closer to him, ready to raise it and swing.

"Con? That you, buddy?"

Jonah's voice startled him so bad that he almost dropped the log. His head swam with questions, and then it hit him.

I'm not at my cabin.

Con could remember the trek here, but had no memory of anything after Doc coming after him outside. Sometime after the German Shepherd's attack, Jonah must have intervened and gotten him to safety. Which meant...

"Noro?" Con croaked. The Heeler whined but stopped moving. She had to be fairly close to him, but he couldn't make out her shape in the darkness.

"No..." Jonah's voice sounded concerned.

"Not *you*." Con turned toward Jonah, who sounded like he was in the kitchen. "I heard her and thought... you know..."

"Ah."

The wind gusted outside, shaking the windows in their frames. A cold chill ran up Con's spine and he pulled the blanket around him, the log still in his lap.

"How much is out there now?"

The darkness made Jonah's hesitation seem longer than it was. "Don't know. The snowfall is slowing down, but visibility is still pretty shit. Maybe two and a half?"

"Jesus. Any luck with the CB?"

"No," Jonah said, almost bitterly. Con could imagine the expression on the man's face: pensive and frustrated, mostly with himself. "Doc's still... out there. Once the snow stops coming down so hard, I'll brave the storm. But it's a little more complicated than I thought."

"How's that?" Con's throat hurt like he'd swallowed glass shards, and his head hurt right behind his left eye. He distantly wondered how high his fever was.

"Power's out—and the gennie's in the shed."

"Oh."

In the darkness, Con found himself staring toward the door. It was still dark outside, but a dim glow illuminated the night. It wasn't enough to see anything in the cabin, but granted an ethereal appearance to the warring environment outside.

Another wave of nausea hit him.

"You have any water?"

"Yeah, one sec."

Con listened as Jonah's heavy boots echoed off the hard floor. He tracked his neighbor's movements, imagining him entering the kitchen with his arms outstretched as he searched for the pantry door. Eventually, it creaked open and the sounds of bags rustling and cans scraping across the shelves filled the cabin.

The steps began to grow closer then, and Con felt a moment of panic. *What if it isn't Jonah?* He imagined his neighbor slowly coming into view as he neared the wood stove, covered in blood the same way Doc had been.

His hand gravitated toward the log and it took everything Con had inside of him not to grip it.

When Jonah finally did reach him, he was relieved to see that his friend was fine. There was no sign that anything at all was wrong, except for the haunted expression the man wore.

"Here."

Con took the jug of water and opened it with shaking hands. He took two or three long sips before pulling it away from his lips with a grimace. His stomach churned at the sudden change. "Do you have a flashlight?" He asked as he handed it back to Jonah, who put the cap onto it and walked it back to the kitchen counter.

"Yeah, but I don't know how long the batteries will last. It's old as dirt and..."

"I need to use the bathroom," Con said quickly. "It'll just be a second."

Jonah seemed to consider as he returned to Con. "If you hand me the log."

For a moment, Con wasn't sure what he meant. Then he remembered the log—the one he'd been very aware of moments before—and fought back against a pang of fear at the idea that something was very wrong with him.

Handing over the log, he took the flashlight from Jonah and tried to stand. His leg immediately protested, and he would have fallen had his neighbor not grabbed his arm.

"Here, come on." The two of them made their way to the bathroom using its dim beam to lead the way. The door was barely shut between them before Con collapsed in front of the toilet and looked back.

"Can you give me some space? I don't mean to be an asshole but..."

A moment of hesitation. "Yeah, man. Sorry."

Con listened as Jonah's footsteps faded. As soon as he thought his friend was far enough away, he vomited so violently that he was sure his throat was bleeding.

The act took everything out of him. He'd had the flu a few years back, but that was nothing compared to this. The body aches, the chills, and the nausea were turned up ten-fold with whatever was happening here. He worried he was legitimately dying.

As soon as he was done, he hung his head down in the space between the cabinet and the toilet. It smelled faintly of piss and household cleaners, a combination that made his stomach lurch again. Opening his eyes, he went to throw up again but stopped.

His mouth hung open and his eyes bugged out of his head as he stared into the toilet. His heart felt like it was clogged, pumping furiously to remove whatever blockage was there. A new sheen of sweat broke out on his skin as he stared into the basin.

Dozens of white shapes moved through his bile, blindly searching. He recognized them immediately—he'd seen them falling from Doc's mouth back at the other cabin.

Only this time, they'd come out of *his* mouth.

Reaching for the handle, he prayed that Jonah hadn't used

the toilet since the power went out. If he had, there would be no water in the tank to flush down the dirty little secret he had expelled from his stomach. His hand shook so violently that it took a couple of tries to flush the toilet, but when he pulled down on the silver handle, the sound of rushing water greeted him.

"Oh thank God."

As silence returned to the bathroom, a sudden knock came at the door.

"Con? Con, you okay?"

"Uh..." He felt unsteady as leaned back against the wall. "Yeah. Yeah, I'm fine. Just feel a little sick."

"We need to get you some antibiotics for your leg," Jonah said through the door. "Do you need me to come in and..."

"*No!*" Con's voice cracked as he yelled it, but he couldn't help it. He imagined Jonah throwing open the door only to discover a stray white form crawling across the toilet seat. "I mean... I'm sorry, I'm just embarrassed."

The silence that greeted him was almost as horrifying as what he'd just expelled from his body. If his neighbor thought something was seriously wrong with him—in a manner that endangered both Jonah and his dog—Con wasn't sure he knew how the man would react.

He'll throw you out with Doc. That's what he'll do.

It sounded like Con's voice, but unfamiliar at the same time, like it had before. He pushed the thought away and stared at the door intently, willing Jonah to say something.

"Okay... whenever you're ready to come out, just let me know."

"Okay. Thank you, Jonah."

The footsteps sounded again, heading away from the door. The urge to vomit hit him again, and it took everything he had to stop himself. As much as he wanted to try to rid himself of the foreign invaders, he would leave evidence behind that they'd been inside him to begin with.

If he knows they're in here, he'll put a bullet in you before you come back.

If Jonah knew he was infected, Con knew what would happen. He had to figure out how to get them out of him before it came to that.

Chapter Eighteen

The first light of dawn seeped through the clouds and still falling snow, creeping over the snowcapped treeline like a creature in search of shelter. It flowed through the window and immediately hit Jonah in the face, waking him from an incoherent nightmare about his wife.

Sitting up, he looked toward Con's still form by the stove. At his feet, Noro snored gently as he noticed the chilly temperature inside the cabin. The heat had drained from the room sometime since he'd fallen asleep, and he rubbed his arms in an effort to warm them. His breath didn't mist out in front of him, but he was sure that his home was only a few degrees away from that milestone.

He cast a glance out at the falling snow—now just coming down at a normal pace—and wondered if he'd waited long enough. The wind still howled outside, masking any other sounds that might be there, but he hoped that Doc would be gone now. The cold was so intense outside of the walls that there was no way the dog could have survived out there in the freezing temperatures.

It wasn't like he had much of a choice anyway. There was no more wood to feed the stove, and he had to keep Con warm long enough until help came. Jonah was already deeply concerned about infection, but he imagined that Con could easily go into shock after so much blood loss.

First thing's first, I need to get to the shed. Start the generator, grab some wood, and get back in here. Then, I go after the CB.

The fear he felt as he climbed into his snow gear was more intense than anything he'd ever experienced. It had been bad enough the night before, but after having faced Doc and seen what the Shepherd was capable of, his anxiety was multiplied ten-fold.

He'd hit the German Shepherd square in the back with a round from his rifle and it had only slowed the dog down for a moment. If Doc was still out there...

Deciding it was best not to think about it anymore, he pulled on his boots and retrieved the rifle. His eyes darted to Con and he considered if he should wake his neighbor. The fever rolling off of the man had been so intense that it had made Jonah sweat when helping to and from the bathroom. He decided to let Con sleep and hope for the best.

He made his way to the back door and cast a look back at Noro, who was still laying by the couch but was now awake. Her ears were perked up as her eyes carefully watched her master.

"I'll be back soon, girl," Jonah said, and hoped he was telling the truth. The deadbolt was cold against his fingers as he turned it slowly. It slid out of place silently, and he slowly eased the door open.

The back of the cabin was still bathed in shadow, but there was nowhere for Doc to hide. The snow back here was a solid sheet, and the woods were a dozen yards away.

Jonah took a deep breath to settle his nerves and pulled the door shut behind him. He was on hyper alert as he stepped off the small platform and made his way down the couple of wooden stairs, his legs sinking into snow above his knees. The powder on top was light and dry, thankfully, but the density of the bottom layer was hard to push through. It took him entirely too long to get to the shed attached to the cabin.

When he finally reached the door, he came to a stop as he realized the problem at hand. The door swung outward—and there was almost three feet of snow blocking it from opening.

"Fuck."

Jonah cast a careful look around the back yard and swallowed hard. The last thing he wanted was to have to be out here longer than what it would take to start the generator and grab a pile of wood, but he knew that he didn't have any choice. He could retreat back to the cabin and burn furniture, but it was a temporary fix. He was still worried about fumes, and it would do nothing to getting him closer to finding help for Con.

Pulling his gloves out of his pocket, he slid his hands into them and began to dig at the snow in front of the door. He was already sweating from anxiety, but soon his undershirt was soaked with it as he frantically pulled the snow away from the shed with his hands.

Come on, come on.

The wind whistled around the sides of the house, and every sound Jonah heard sent his heart speeding. He imagined Doc, nearly frozen solid with a snarl frozen on its broken snout, appearing around the side of the shed.

If that happened, there wouldn't be enough time to grab his rifle off his shoulder and aim it. The German Shepherd would get to him long before he could.

When the snow was finally cleared enough and Jonah pulled the door open enough to squeeze in, he let out a sigh of relief. The interior of the shed was pitch black, the only light inside of it coming from the crack in the slightly ajar door.

His heart raced as he pulled the rifle off of his shoulder and leaned it against the wall by the door. The space inside was small, and it didn't take him long to locate the generator in the back of it by memory alone. He blindly felt his way around the blocky frame until his fingers found the pull cord.

Grabbing it, he yanked on it hard. The generator tried to turn over but sputtered near the end. Jonah cursed and planted one boot on the edge of it, gripping the cord with both hands. After a deep breath, he pulled with all of his might.

The motor caught this time, but the motion sent him falling backward. He hit the ground hard and his head turned toward the open door as he landed.

Doc's teeth snapped shut a mere inch from his face—if the Shepherd's snout hadn't been broken, Jonah would have lost his nose. He screamed in terror and rolled into the woodpile directly opposite of the door, pushing himself against it as tightly as his body would allow.

With each lunge, Doc tried to squeeze further into the shed. The dog's hair, wet with blood and melted snow, pulled out as it tried to reach Jonah. Its fur was wet with melted snow and blood.

His eyes gravitated toward the gun leaning right next to the door.

"Oh fuck, oh fuck," Jonah choked out between shallow breaths. His heart hammered like it was about to give out as Doc's shoulders thumped against the door and the frame again and again.

The snow must have fallen back down behind it after I came in. It was a small mercy, but one that had allowed him to live for to this point. If the door had been able to open as wide as it had been when he squeezed through it, Doc wouldn't have missed that first time.

As he watched, he swore that the German Shepherd was inching closer. Jonah raised his booted foot and kicked out as hard as he could. His blow landed square between the undead dog's eyes with a sickening crunch. If Doc felt anything, there was no sign.

Doc lunged again, and Jonah was sure of it now: the Shepherd was almost into the shed. Panic took hold and he debated going after the rifle. The only thing that stopped him was remembering Con's leg and his mysterious fever.

Using the wood pile, he pulled himself to his feet. Logs fell from the stack behind him, hitting the floor and rolling...

One of them came to a stop against the rusty head of his axe. He'd forgotten it was even in here—it had come with the cabin when he and Diane had bought it, and he'd never had to use it.

Until now.

Grabbing it, Jonah brought it up and held it so the head was parallel with his shoulder. His hands, still inside the glittens, gripped the handle clumsily as he watched Doc squirm and slam against the door and the frame. The Shepherd was nearly half-way in now, and it would only be another moment before it was fully inside the shed.

Jonah raised the axe and let out a guttural scream full of terror as he brought it down with as much force as he could. He aimed at the base of Doc's neck, and he fully expected to hear a yelp of pain when the blade connected. His stomach clenched with guilt and disgust at the thought of it.

The German Shepherd made no sound. The head of the axe connected, sliding through Doc's thick neck. Jonah pulled back at the last second before it hit, but the damage was considerable. As he yanked the axe out of Doc, the dog collapsed onto the floor of the shed and lay twitching.

Bile rose in Jonah's throat and he vomited onto the floor beside the generator, bracing himself against the shed for support. All he could imagine was Noro laying there instead of Doc, and it tore him to pieces.

The fine grey hairs on the back of his neck rose and a deep dread expelled the residual fear and fresh guilt from his mind.

Turning, he watched as Doc's partially decapitated body tried to rise from the floor. Its legs twitched and spazzed, sliding out from underneath it as it attempted to get back up. Doc's one remaining eye, filmy white, rolled in its socket.

"Jesus fucking Christ," Jonah said, slowly reaching for the axe he'd dropped.

The dog suddenly twisted toward him, pushing itself around the floor like a baby trying to learn to crawl.

Jonah picked up the axe and backed up until the back of his legs knocked against the running generator. His hands were slick with sweat inside his glittens, and he gripped the handle so hard that his knuckled popped.

There was no blood on the floor as Doc inched across it. The memory of Con's words flashed through Jonah's mind: *he was sweating blood*. There was nothing left inside of the German Shepherd.

Jonah prepared to strike, working up the nerve to bring the axe down one more time, when Doc finally grew still. The seconds stretched on as he waited for Doc to rise one more time like a horror movie villain, but it never came. The German Shepherd remained unmoving.

After what felt like an eternity, Jonah lowered the axe and used the head of it to prod Doc's lifeless body. When there was no reaction, he did it again, but harder.

Doc's head slid to the side, revealing the raw meat where

the axe had partially severed it. A white shape that looked like a bone protruded from it, stark against the already decaying flesh. His hand was shaking so badly that he could barely hold the axe steady as he slowly poked the white protrusion.

The white shape pulled away at the touch, disappearing into the meat with a sickening squelching sound.

Jonah stumbled backward, falling on top of the running generator and dropping the axe. A scream escaped his throat as he stared at Doc's body with eyes so wide that his eyelids spasmed.

As he watched, the white shape reappeared at the same spot. He could see it slowly turning in place, as if searching for something, and then it began to slide out of its place.

He remembered another thing that Con had said: *it got inside of him.* The white, worm-like creature slowly slithered from Doc's corpse and landed on the hard floor of the shed. It was nearly a foot long and legless, without any sort of determinable features that Jonah could make out.

It coiled into itself like a snake before one end of it slowly rose in the air. Jonah's breath puffed out in front of him, coming quicker and quicker. The parasite—for that was surely what he was looking at—pointed in his direction. A low hiss emitted from it as the smooth white surface of its underbelly separated, revealing rows upon rows of barbed teeth. Pieces of Doc's vertebrae still clung to some of them.

"Oh, fuck *this.*"

Jonah pulled himself up and ran for the door as the parasite lunged. Its teeth seemed impossibly large as it narrowly missed him. Grabbing the gun, he turned and aimed it at the thick, tubular creature that lay on the floor.

It turned back toward him, flashing those teeth. Jonah didn't hesitate; he pulled the trigger. The sound was deafening in the small space, but the effect of the round itself was much larger. It caught the parasite dead in its center, obliterating it in a spray of green gore and chunks of white flesh. Its barbed teeth sprayed like shrapnel, spraying the floors and walls with a sound like someone dropping a can of nails.

As the ringing in his ears subsided, he was left only with the hum of the generator and his own ragged breathing.

It's over, he thought with a wild sort of relief. *It's fucking over.*

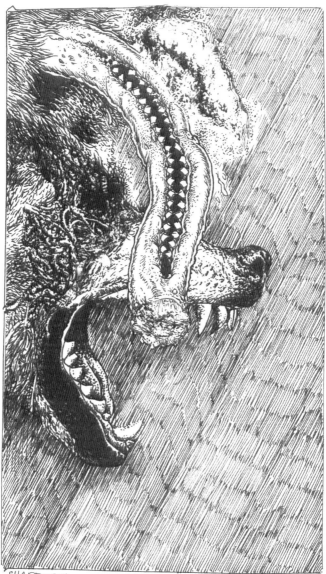

CHADBOURNE

Chapter Nineteen

It moved inside Con's stomach. The sensation drew a faint memory from many years ago of pressing a small hand to the belly of his pregnant aunt as she declared: *"I felt it kick, I felt it kick!"*

This was entirely different though. The way his stomach bulged and protruded as it turned inside of him inspired fear, not joy. He could still hear Doc's ribs breaking as it worked its way though the Shepherd's body, looking for its home at the base of his dog's skull.

There is no other way.

The voice was emotionless and spoke with perfect diction. He wondered how he could have ever confused it as his own, but chalked it up to the fever that was still burning its way through his body. His cells must be baking, dying of the extreme heat generated as his immune system fought this foreign invader.

Across the room, Noro whined and backed up closer to Jonah's bedroom while Con tossed and turned.

It is nearly time.

"Fuck you."

A searing pain exploded in Con's abdomen, causing him to bite back a scream. Outside, all he could hear was the wind whistling around the side of the house.

"*Jonah!*"

There was no answer besides a single, high pitched bark from Noro. If his neighbor was anywhere inside the cabin, Con didn't know where.

The pain intensified as he climbed off the mattress and stumbled into the kitchen. His ruined leg was nothing compared to the agony he was experiencing inside of him. It was like someone had taken a hot knife and—

The generator roared to life outside, causing several lights in the cabin to turn on.

He's outside, Con and the parasite thought simultaneously.

Making his way into the kitchen, Con threw himself against the counter as another wave of excruciating pain tore through his midsection. The image of the way the parasite inside of Doc had wormed its way through the dog's body played on repeat.

How did it even get inside of me?

He knew the answer, even though he wished he didn't. The bite. Doc's mouth had been spilling over with larvae during his horrific death and eventual resurrection, so it bore to reason that some of them had gotten into this body when the Shepherd's jaws clamped down on his leg.

Con turned on the stovetop and watched as the fire burst to life with the familiar hiss of gas. It was a good thing that Jonah had never tried to update the cabin's amenities, because an electric stove wouldn't have worked as well for what he was about to do.

He twisted his body and reached for the handle of a knife sticking out of a block situated on the counter. His fingers closed around the smooth black plastic and he pulled the butcher's blade out. The stainless steel flashed in the light from the windows and the overhead lights.

"Okay, Con."

That isn't going to work.

"You can do this. Don't be a chickenshit." As he spoke, the only thing shaking worse than his voice was his hand as he held the blade over the open flame. "It's just like dressing a deer."

Only I'm the deer.

Con knew there was a very high likelihood that he was going to die trying to cut this thing out of him. It was a better fate than the alternative, though.

From across the room, Noro whined. Con turned toward her and felt a pang of guilt. If what he was about to failed and that thing got out...

Con made his way across the room, leaving the knife on the counter. His bad leg dragged against the floor as he limped toward Noro, who retreated backward until she was all the way into Jonah's bedroom. The air was now so cold that Con could see his breath puffing out in front of him as he stopped in the doorway.

"Good girl, Noro."

There was a dresser beside the door. Con opened one of the drawers and pulled out three pairs of long thermal pants before reaching for the door handle. A sudden pang of agony nearly doubled him over as he turned the lock on the handle and shut it behind him, sealing Noro in the bedroom.

Next, he dropped all three thermals and used his bad leg to push them into the crack at the bottom of the door. It wasn't perfect but it was better than nothing.

Returning to the counter, Con stuck the blade back into the fire and waited. The pain was growing more severe and coming in quicker intervals.

You can't wait any longer, he told himself as he pulled the butcher knife out of the flame. *You have to do it now.*

The voice, cold and so sure: *you can try.*

Con took the knife and slit his shirt open with a shaking hand. The skin there was mottled with bruises from the movement of the parasite inside of him. His breathing quickened as he changed his grip on the knife and tried to remember anything he could from high school biology.

There was nothing there, so he decided to wing it.

God, please help me.

The knife slid into his skin, causing him to cry out as he cut his midsection open. It hurt so badly that he almost collapsed, but he remained standing at full height. He figured it would be harder to dig the thing out of him if he was hunched over.

Blood poured down his navel and across the front of his pants as he cut. He didn't know exactly what he was cutting, only that he had to get to his stomach.

I'm literally killing myself.

The fever that burned away at his body had affected his decision-making skills. There was no way he was going to survive cutting himself open. They were stranded out in the woods with an out of date first aid kit and no way to call for help.

He told himself that it was a better fate than letting this thing inside of him pilot his body. He was dead either way, he realized now—but this way, he at least got to have control over his final moments and what happened after. The last act he would commit would be to slice the parasite inside of him in half.

After what seemed like forever, he switched the knife to his left hand. The entire front of his lower half was coated with blood that pooled at his bare feet. He refused to look down out of fear of losing his resolve. He could feel the parasite moving around inside his stomach, but it must have stopped burrowing because the pain had subsided.

Either that, or he was in shock.

Closing his eyes, he slowly stuck his shaking right hand inside the long incision in his torso. The feeling was indescribable. In his youth, he'd been to many Halloween parties with bowls full of different things that claimed to be eyeballs, tongues, and guts, but the truth was that none of them had even come close to capturing what it was really like. His fingers numbly poked at his intestines. The blood made them feel like thick, algae covered rope as he searched,

Finally, his finger tips poked against something that pushed back.

There.

His left hand was shaking so badly that he cut his fingers several times before the tip of the knife found what he hoped was the lining of his stomach. The point slipping in, cutting away at the tissue there.

The parasite squirmed and rotated, trying to escape. Before it could do anything, Con dug his fingers into the hole he'd cut into his stomach and closed them around the tubular creature.

"God, please help me..."

He began to pull, but the parasite resisted. A different pain erupted from his stomach, similar to the cramps he'd had after eating meat that had gone bad but ten thousand times worse. He fought through it, trying not to think about what could be causing it. The piece of the parasite he held began to move, pushing against his grip.

"What the..."

Dozens of sharp pangs of pain erupted from his hand as he cried out. He couldn't help it now—he looked down and gasped.

About seven inches of the parasite was out of his torso, but there was still more coming. Smaller larvae fell onto the floor the body of the larger one, landing in the pool of blood there. As Con watched, the tubular creature opened down an invisible seam. Rows of sharp, barbed teeth revealed themselves as it tried desperately to free itself from Con's grip.

"You... aren't... getting..."

A gunshot tore through the wind outside, catching Con off guard. His feet moved, stepping fully into the puddle of blood he stood in. The slick substance robbed him of his balance and he found himself sliding. The knife clattered from his grip as he struggled to find his footing. His now free hand went to the counter but it was too late.

His feet slipped out from under him and he went down hard. His head slammed against the counter with a crack and everything went dark.

* * *

As Con's lifeless body lay on the ground, the parasite slowly slid from his now loose grip and disappeared back into the ragged cut across his chest. Con's body shifted ever so slightly as it slowly broke through the wall of his esophagus and wormed its way through his ribs. His cut shirt was pulled away from his back, and the shape of the parasite was clear as it worked its way up his spine toward the base of his skull.

When it finally reached its destination, Con's body remained still for a very long time. Outside, the wind rose in speed and volume, masking Noro's anxious whines from behind Jonah's locked door. She dug at the crack at the base of the door in a desperate attempt to get free.

Con's limbs spasmed as if his body had been touched with a live wire. It happened half a dozen times, and then his fingers slowly started to move. They were slow, clunky actions that grew finer with each passing second.

Overhead, footsteps on the roof echoed through the quiet cabin.

Con sat upright, blood caked to the side of his head. Turning his head upward, he stared for a long time as the footsteps made their way to the edge of the roof.

Con tried to smile, but the muscles of his face wouldn't work the way the creature desired. What came out was an approximation of a grin, twisted and crooked without any real humor or joy.

"Joe-nuh?"

Chapter Twenty

The snow on the roof was hard to move through, but Jonah didn't have time to shovel it off. It had been hard to climb onto the roof from the shorter shed, but he'd just barely managed it after his close encounter with the parasite.

Even now, the image of its many barbed teeth haunted him. His heart raced at the thought of it.

You should have taken the wood in first. Got the fire going and—

As much as Jonah desired to get the cabin warmed up, he knew that Con's medical condition was the most dire thing right now. He needed to get the CB hooked up and make the call to get help before he did anything.

The antenna stuck out of the snow like a beacon. The black coaxial cable still hung on it, over one hundred feet long, shaking in the high winds that threatened to toss Jonah off the roof.

He chastised himself again for not hooking it up. Con had gone through all the trouble of getting it for him, and he'd been so arrogant that he'd believed he wouldn't need it. All it would have taken was an hour of his time and a drill to get it functioning, and Con would already be getting the help he needed.

Reaching the antenna, Jonah extended his arm and grabbed the cable. His exposed fingers were cold, but he couldn't connect the coaxial cable with them covered. The insulation around the cable was stiff and it took a long time to unroll it, but Jonah managed. The snow was barely falling now, but the sun still hid behind grey clouds. It would be a long time before all of it melted, and Jonah couldn't wait to see the ground again.

He figured it was likely that this would be his last day at the cabin—he would take Noro and set up shop somewhere warmer. Fuck the finances; he'd figure it out.

Jonah grabbed one end of the cable and began to search for the antenna mount to connect it to. After searching the upper part, he began to dig the snow away from its base. He found it quickly, and uttered a quick thanks to Con. If the man hadn't been so absolutely relentless with his questioning and his directions, Jonah would likely have no idea what he was doing. As it stood, he remembered pretty much everything Con had told him.

Screwing the coaxial cable into the mount, Jonah grabbed the other end and walked it back to the shed. He tossed it into the snow beside the back door before climbing down onto the roof of the shed and back down to the ground.

The wind whipped snow into the air as Jonah stepped back into the shed. He had to sidestep Doc's body, an act that gave him great anxiety and guilt, but he had to retrieve his gun and the wood.

The parasite still lay on the ground where he'd shot it. As far as he could tell, it hadn't moved a millimeter from where he'd left it. What was left of it lay in a puddle of dark green, viscous fluid. Its teeth were scattered across the shed, with some even embedded in the walls.

Jonah hurriedly slung the rifle over his shoulder and grabbed a couple of pieces of firewood from the pile. Tucking the wood under his left arm, he exited the shed and made his way to where he'd thrown the coaxial cable. After picking it up, he pushed through the snow to the cabin and climbed the stairs to the back door.

When Jonah threw open the door, he was surprised that Noro didn't greet him. Her absence immediately made him feel uneasy, and he grew more uncomfortable once he saw how dark the cabin was.

Why the hell did he close the curtains? Jonah flipped the switch for the kitchen light. When it didn't turn on, he became deeply afraid.

Setting down the wood and the cable at the door, he unslung his rifle and gripped it with both hands.

"Con? Noro?"

The only response he got was a single, high pitched bark from his room. *What the fuck is she doing in there?*

"Con? Where the hell are you, man?"

Jonah stepped into the dark cabin, his eyes searching the gloom for any sign of Con. He wasn't exactly sure what he was expecting, but he knew that something was very wrong.

Maybe the circuit breaker box just needs reset.

It was a possibility. The sudden outage could have tripped the breakers. It was an old cabin, after all, but it still didn't explain Con's absence.

What if Con's already dead?

It was a horrible thought, but one that Jonah knew was likely. Immense guilt, as familiar as a long-time lover, washed over him. *This is my fault.*

The breaker box was at the other end of the living room. As

Jonah passed the island, he cast a careful glance at the mattress Con had been sleeping in. It was still incredibly dark, but he could clearly see that his neighbor wasn't there. His eyes shifted to the bathroom.

Maybe there?

Instead of checking, Jonah went for the curtains first. Pulling them open, he found himself looking at the empty living room. Con's blankets lay in a heap beside the mattress, but there was no sign of the man himself.

You need to keep your head on straight, Jonah told himself. He had to get the power on before he did anything, because otherwise the CB wouldn't even work. Above anything else, he needed to call for help.

He crossed the living room quickly, his fear mounting despite the increased light in the room. To his surprise, the breaker box was already opened when he reached it. Jonah lowered his rifle and reached out, feeling the different breakers. All of the were switched to on except one: the master.

Something was deeply wrong. This wasn't done by the storm—the master had clearly been turned off by someone.

Jonah flipped the breaker back to on. The sudden presence of the warm glow of lightbulbs brought him more comfort than he would have thought, but only for a moment.

His eyes fell on the kitchen floor and his mouth went dry. The floor was covered in just as much blood as Con's had been, maybe even more so. It pooled on the hardwood and reflected the light from the overhead bulbs. Bloody handprints decorated the counter in several places, like art left behind.

"Oh God..."

Jonah's eyes moved to Con's mattress, which was soaked in blood where the man had been laying. When Con had told him about Doc's demise, he'd said the dog was sweating blood— which seemed impossible, because dogs don't sweat—but now

Jonah had a feeling that Con had been right, he'd just called it the wrong thing.

He took a step forward, raising his rifle. There was no sign of Con anywhere. His eyes zeroed in on the bathroom door, and he started toward it. The temperature in the cabin was plummeting now; he'd left the back door open for light, but now it was freezing inside the small home.

"Con? Con, are you in there?"

There was no reply. Jonah swallowed hard and leaned forward, pressing the barrel of the rifle on the slightly ajar bathroom door. Pushing it, he backed away quickly. The light from the main room flooded the bathroom, illuminating what little of the space he could see. Part of him had expected to find Con standing right behind the door, waiting for him. The relief he felt was immense.

It was also short-lived.

As he took another step back, Con lunged from behind the other side of the island. It was maybe a yard between Jonah and the man, but the man moved so fast that the knife was slicing through Jonah's Achilles tendon before he realized what was happening.

A cry of agony erupted from Jonah as he fell sideways, dropping the rifle as he his arms came up to protect his face. His aging body landed on the floor hard, knocking the breath out of him and surely breaking a few ribs for good measure.

"*Ah, fuck!*"

Inside the bedroom, Noro began to bark furiously. Con stood as Jonah's hands cradled his injured ankle. The way his neighbor rose from the floor was like something out of a horror movie: joints jutting at odd angles as he tried to figure out how they were supposed to move to accommodate his intent.

It's too late.

"Con..."

One of them is inside of him.

Then: *There's more than one...*

"...listen, man..."

Don't try to reason with it.

"... you don't have to do this."

Con's head cocked inquisitively, but his neck craned too far. His ear nearly rested on his shoulder, giving him a nearly comical appearance. No one was laughing though.

The urge to vomit was almost too powerful as Jonah saw the damage Con had inflicted upon himself, no doubt trying to rid himself of the horrendous invader inside of him. His torso was cut from sternum to navel, hanging open and revealing a mess of severed intestines and other organs that hung from the hole.

"Jesus..."

"A... tall-tale... told by... humans... to... comfort... themselves," Con croaked suddenly, his voice rising and falling in volume and octave with each word. It was like he was learning to speak all over again. *Or for the first time.*

"What?" Jonah sputtered. Blood pooled in his snow pants and leaked out of the bottom and through the slit that Con had created.

"Jesus... *Christ!*" Con nearly screamed the last word, his voice shrill and ear-splitting. "Is... a... tall-tale..."

It was like watching a child answer a question posed in a classroom. The thing in control of Con was spouting facts that it was pulling out of his mind in response to Jonah's words.

"Why are you doing this?" His words cut off Con's question. The same inquisitive lean of his head followed as he searched Jonah's face for something.

"This... is... how... we... survive."

Jonah swallowed hard as he scooted along the floor to his gun. He was hyper-aware that Con stood with weight distributed evenly on both legs despite his injury, and even more so of the knife that Con clasped.

"We... must find... *hosts?*" He turned the last word into a question, as if unsure if it was the right fit. "We cannot... live on our own."

The diction was becoming clearer and more evened out the more Con talked. With each passing phrase, his tone found a natural cadence. It was vastly unlike Con's real voice, but there were hints of it there.

"You killed him."

"Yes."

The simplicity of the answer stunned Jonah as his fingers brushed the stock of his rifle. "What do you want here?"

"To survive." Con moved with freakish speed toward Jonah without warning, his limbs flailing in an exaggerated fashion. Landing on top of him, he pressed the knife to Jonah's throat. "For my children to survive."

"Children?" Jonah choked out. The blade of the knife was unbelievably sharp against his neck.

Con's face grew perplexed—the most realistic human expression Jonah had seen the parasite mimic yet. "Of course. What is the purpose of life, but to create and continue it?"

A rather profound question, Jonah thought, but then Con vomited into his face before he could get the words out to say so.

Bile rose in Jonah's throat in response and he shoved Con as hard as he could, be damned with the knife. A slit throat was the least of his problems now. Small, tiny organisms moved on his face, probing for some sort of entry point as the knife nicked his neck as it fell away from him. Con landed on the ground hard but didn't cry out.

Jonah rolled onto his stomach and began to wipe fero-ciously as his cheeks and forehead with his gloved hands.

When he pulled it away, he found dozens of white, maggot-looking parasites wriggling against the wool. Pulling the gloves off, he continued to try to rid himself of the unwelcome visitors. He quickly realized he was in a losing battle. One of them wormed its way up his nose, forcing him to blow it out like a snot-rocket. It collided with the floor and lay there, moving back and forth. Another found its way in at the corner of his mouth; a third neared the corner of his eye. Still, he fought and fought until his hands came away without any more white, twitching shapes.

"You are now one of us, Jonah."

Con's voice, proper and without the backwoods cadence that had characterized it before, stoked a furious rage in him.

"Fuck you."

Jonah was still near the rifle. Diving for it, he rolled onto his back and pointed the barrel straight at Con's face. He pulled the trigger and watched as everything from the nose up disintegrated in a cloud of gore. The man stumbled backward but did not drop—instead, he began to blindly shuffle toward Jonah, his legs barely moving as he dragged one foot after the other.

"Jo-ah..." The monstrous site before him managed to say. The top of his jaw hung crooked, revealing a bulging tongue trying to speak.

Jonah chambered another round, feeling his heart beating wildly. The corpse before him stumbled forward, now nearly on top of him. Raising the rifle, he fired another shot, this time at Con's neck.

The rest of Con's head disappeared. His teeth made a sound eerily similar to that of the parasite's outside as they exploded outward. The ringing in Jonah's ears was horrendous, but he heard that just fine.

Con stopped moving as he stood above Jonah, now just a headless corpse that swayed back and forth. His—*its*—knees locked before loosening and then locking again as the parasite tried its best to manipulate the body.

It doesn't know how.

Con's memories were gone; they were little more than chunks of grey matter that decorated the walls of Jonah's cabin now. The parasite didn't have anything to reference. What little that must have remained after the first round was obliterated by the second. At this point, Con's body was just a puppet with too many strings.

The knife fell from Con's hand and stuck in the floor by Jonah's left thigh.

Jonah was about to slide backwards but stopped as he watched one of the most horrific sights yet. The parasite began to pull out of the ragged stump where Con's face used to be. While the other one had only been about a foot long, Jonah could already see at least two feet of this one. It was twice as thick as the other one too, resembling a telephone line more than a rope.

When Con's knees began to shake, he realized a second too late what was about to happen. The corpse before him moved forward with sudden speed, dropping on top of him with enough force to knock the wind out of him.

As he lay gasping for air, the parasite rose up—part of it still inside of Con's body—and opened up like the other one had. Jonah's right arm flew up without a second to spare. The creature slammed down, its dozens of gnashing teeth intended for Jonah's face, and instead found his forearm. The teeth immediately pierced his jacket and bit into his skin, the barbed ends sinking deep into his flesh. Another scream erupted from him as the parasite tugged, trying to free itself to strike again.

Jonah's left hand reached for the knife, stretching as far as he could. Con's body pinned him to the ground, limiting his range of motion, but it was close. His fingers brushed against the handle as the parasite finally yanked itself free, pulling chunks of muscle and flesh with it. It took everything that Jonah had to not grab his injured arm and cradle it, but he managed. His left hand wrapped around the handle as the creature came down again, biting into his left arm near the elbow this time.

Screaming, Jonah pulled the knife out of the floor. His next move was excruciating but satisfying.

He pulled his arm free of the thing's freakish jowls. As soon as it was off of him, his left hand grabbed the parasite's head. He growled against the pain as the barbed teeth bit into his palm.

"Survive this."

Jonah swung the knife as hard as he could, slicing through the parasite right where above where it exited Con's neck. It writhed in his grip, squeezing its rows of teeth together in its death throes.

Pushing Con's body off of him, he rolled over and threw the parasite as hard as he could against the wood stove. It hit the cast-iron and dropped onto the stone below it, unmoving.

He lay there for a while, breathing heavily and feeling every pain in his body. His broken ribs, his injured left arm, his severed tendon—they all paled in comparison to what he knew was the real threat. Pushing himself to his feet, he knew that he didn't have much time.

Chapter Twenty-One

J onah hobbled to the pile of the wood and leaned against the door frame as he reached down and picked them up. Tossing them toward the stove one after the other, he made his way across the living room on one leg.

It took very little time to get a roaring fire going in the stove. The orange flames gave off a comforting warmth that did little to ease his worries. He kept waiting for some sign of fever or abdominal pain, but nothing had hit yet. It had taken Con very little time to begin to show symptoms, but Jonah had no idea if it had been because of the bite or the parasite.

Before he closed the door, Jonah made sure to pick up the lifeless creature that lay beside it. It hung in his hand, as if it were no more threatening than a piece of rope. He threw it into the stove as hard as he could and slammed it shut, locking it.

Next, he made his way back to the open door. The coaxial cable still sat there, as if mocking him. All of this could have been avoided if he had taken things more seriously—the second time such a thing could have made a huge difference.

Diane.

He hoped she would be waiting for him at the end. Maybe it was wishful thinking for a man who hadn't believed in Heaven since he was little, but it was a comforting thought.

The rest of the CB radio setup had been done by Con at his house the day he'd given it to Jonah. *Shit's just plug and play— so plug it in, and play with it.* The phantom voice of his neighbor struck a chord within him, almost making him cry. He'd been harsh to Con, unfair even; and Con had nothing but a good friend to him.

His best friend, even.

"I'm sorry for being an old asshole," Jonah muttered as he shut the door as tightly as the cable would allow. Limping across the room and using the wall for support, he looked behind the radio base. The power cord was already plugged in, but the speaker's cables still hung loose behind it. He carefully plugged them in with trembling hands, then screwed the coaxial cable into place.

Moment of truth.

Jonah flipped the on switch, and the LED screen came to life with a burst of static through the speakers. He picked up the dynamic microphone and clicked the button before remembering to change the channel. Con had written the emergency channel in black magic marker on the top of the radio: a sloppy nine that hung lopsided.

It took him a minute to figure out how to move from channel to channel, but he figured it out. Once the LED display read "nine," Jonah lifted the microphone to his lips and hit the button.

"My name is Jonah Miller. I live at 19338 Prairie Way, up on the mountain. I have a medical emergency, and need help immediately."

There was a long moment of silence where he thought that maybe he'd set it up wrong or, worse, no one was listening. Then the crackle as someone joined the channel.

"Mr. Miller? You still there? Over."

* * *

After cutting the coaxial cable and shutting the door tight, Jonah had one last thing to do before leaving the cabin. The stove was stocked full and he hoped that it would last long enough until help arrived. His last responsibility was the most painful.

Jonah picked the lock to the bedroom door with ease, using a small, flathead screwdriver to turn it. As soon as the door opened, Noro jumped up from her place beside it and barked a single, excited bark.

Shoving the screwdriver into his pocket, he reached down and pulled the large bag of dogfood into the room with Noro.

"Hey girl, I bet you're starving."

Noro saw the bag of food and wagged her tail, but didn't go for it. His heart ached, knowing that she was waiting because she knew not to eat out of the bag.

"Here," Jonah said, reaching down and picking up the bag. While he didn't think his Achilles tendon was fully severed, putting any weight on it was excruciating, but he managed to keep his balance on one leg and lift the dogfood. He turned it over, dumping it onto the floor. As soon as the kibble hit the ground, Noro went after it. "Good girl."

Next, Jonah pulled the mop bucket from under the sink into the room. The fresh, clean water in it sloshed as he scooted it to the wall by the door. He didn't really like the idea of Noro drinking out of it, but on the off chance that she was here for a little longer than he expected, he wanted to make sure she had enough food and water.

He let Noro eat for a moment as he made his way to the bed. Once he was seated on the edge, he whistled to her to come.

She immediately started toward him, moving slowly. He cursed himself for not grabbing one of her pills before coming in, but he couldn't change that. Hopefully help would come soon, and she would be comfortable enough until then.

"Come on, Noro," Jonah said, reaching down and lifting her onto the bed. The act was incredibly painful, aggravating both his bites and his ribs, but it was a necessary agony.

"Listen up, girl." He scratched behind her ears and immediately felt the tears coming. "I know you probably don't understand me, or if you do, you don't understand why. But I've got to go away now, okay?"

The tears broke; tears that had been kept behind a dam since the last day Diane drove off in the Ford Explorer.

"I don't want to leave you. You're my special girl, you know?" Noro licked at his tears, and he struggled to keep his composure. "Thank you, for always behind here. I don't know that I would be here without you—and I intend to repay the favor, okay?

"Be nice to the men that come. Please. They'll take good care of you."

In the still moment that followed, Jonah contemplated.

"I... I never should have let her keep driving that car. I just... I always said it cost a lot of money to replace a fuel pump on an old car like that, and the car wasn't worth half that. Money was never a problem. I knew it, and the kids knew it. I just... didn't think anything would happen.

"Diane's gone because I was selfish. Same with Con. I won't let the same think happen to you.

"I love you, Noro. You're the best dog anyone could ask for; and the best friend."

With that, Jonah told her to stay and stepped out of the room, careful to place the clothes back into the crack.

Just in case.

Epilogue

verett Bailey pulled the plow off of the road and down the long driveway to his destination: Jonah Miller's cabin on Prairie Way. The deep snow flew up in a miniature blizzard as the truck paved the way, the ambulance close behind.

Everett readjusted his trooper hat and swallowed hard. Miller hadn't been exactly forthcoming with information: just that he and his neighbor were in dire need of medical. In the three hours between now and then that it had taken Everett to get up the mountain, there had been no further communication.

His Chevy Colorado came to a stop outside of the cabin after doing a short loop around, making it easier to get out when the time came. The ambulance followed suit, breaking slowly and parking near the porch of the cabin.

The cold air bit at Everett as he climbed out of the truck and pulled his jacket tighter around him. The Wyoming State Police patch on the left arm was coming loose—he'd have to get it mended before long. He turned back toward the ambulance, where two women were climbing out in equally bulky parkas, similar to his own.

"Ev, your people heard anything else from this guy?" Marie asked. Her red hair poked out from underneath her black knit hat, bringing the green out in her eyes.

Everett shook his head. "Checked back with them about a mile back, still radio silent."

"That's great," Hailey, a full two-heads taller than Marie, chimed in. "How do we know this isn't just some crank call bullshit, then? Or worse, some psycho?"

"If it is some lunatic, I would be more scared for him than for you."

"He's got a point there," Marie said as walked to the back of the ambulance and retrieved the duffel full of their supplies. It looked massive on her small shoulders, but Everett never offered to take it from her. He'd learned from experience that both Marie and Hailey were desperate to be taken seriously at what was essentially a boys' party out in rural Wyoming, and he could understand why. Whenever something happened, most of the other officers felt that the two women needed to keep their noses where it belonged. Often the other men stated that was 'out of their business and in the kitchen,' a notion that Everett had reported more than a few of them over. Nothing ever came of it, and nothing ever got better for either of them, but at least he tried. After the third time of inaction, he'd settled for sticking up for them. They were both tough and didn't take shit from anyone and, while that sometimes made his life more difficult, he could respect it.

She slammed the door shut, and a sudden sound filled the silence.

"Is that a dog?" Marie asked.

"If I get bit, I want worker's comp," Hailey said, turning to Everett. "You hear me?"

"If the dog takes a chunk out of your ass, I promise to sign off on whatever you want to say," Everett laughed, walking along the plowed trail until he was standing in front of the porch. "I'm sure it's nothing. Probably slipped and broke his hip or something."

Leading the way, Everett pushed through the thigh high snow and up the porch stairs. Behind him, Hailey cleared the way for Marie and the two of them joined him as he knocked on the door.

"Hello? Mr. Miller, anyone home?" Nothing but the barking dog greeted him. "Okay, well I don't love that," he muttered.

Everett reached for the handle and turned it, unsurprised to find it unlocked. No one this far out seemed too worried about locking their doors, a concept that he hoped someone would not come to regret one day. He pushed the door, only to find something blocking it. Frustration mounting, he put all of his weight against it and felt it give, inch by inch, as a heavy piece of furniture slid out of the way. The door now fully open, he looked inside.

"Holy *shit*," was all Everett managed before rushing to the edge of the porch and throwing up his breakfast. His wife's bacon, eggs, and waffles had been delicious going down, but not so much coming back up. He could hear Hailey and Marie talking as he wiped his mouth with the sleeve of his jacket and pulled his gun. "Stand back."

Everett stepped foot into the cabin, his pistol leveled before him. A pool of blood sat in the middle of the living room. There was gore splattered against the far wall, and he could see from where he stood there was a considerable amount of it in the kitchen as well. A trail led from the pool of blood on the floor to the backdoor, as if something had been dragged outside.

Bits of bone, flesh, and meat the looked suspiciously like organs were scattered across the scene.

He'd never seen anything like it.

Or someone.

"Stay outside," he said over his shoulder. The cabin was small, with only three rooms besides the main one: a bathroom and two bedrooms. Everett cleared the bathroom first, finding it empty. As he crossed the living room, he was careful not to step in any blood. There was a mattress on the floor, and as he passed it he saw there was blood on it as well.

What the hell happened here?

The dog continued to bark from the one bedroom, so Everett checked the other first. There was nothing out of place there, except the missing mattress on the frame. He had no idea why someone would have dragged it out, but they clearly had.

Exiting the room, he turned his attention to the last bedroom. He stepped in front of it and noticed a note pinned to it with a yellow pushpin. Without touching it, Everett read:

> To whom it may concern,
> Inside of this room is Noro. Weird name, I know. My wife wanted to name her Nora, but her handwriting was so bad the license was interpreted as 'Noro,' so it stuck.
> Noro is a good girl. The <u>best</u> girl. She won't bite. She has medicine in the kitchen. By the time you're reading this, she'll likely need a gabapentin. She's getting old.
> My name is Jonah Miller, and I killed my neighbor.

Everett's mouth went dry, but he continued reading.

This story is going to sound crazy, but here goes. Somewhere in the woods surrounding his cabin (just a mile or so west) you'll find a meteor that crashed during the storm. Something came out of it. It got into his dog, then got into him, then got into me.

You'll find very little evidence of this, but for good reason. You'll find the three of us are in the backyard, but it'll be hard to figure out exactly what happened.

All you need to know is that whatever came out of the meteor is gone. You are safe, so please don't leave my dog here.

My son Alex Miller will be happy to take her. Just call him at the number below. And do me a favor? Tell him I'm sorry. He was right.

The letter ended there, without a signature. Everett's head spun as he reread it. He couldn't begin to understand the ramblings of this man, who was clearly insane.

Still, he found himself deeply uneasy as he opened the door a crack. He fully expected to see someone standing there, ready to strike with some twisted looking mask on like in the movies, but instead he was greeted by an aging Blue Heeler.

"Uh... Noro, I presume?"

The Heeler wagged her tail at mention of her name. Everett knelt by the door, his hand still on the handle and ready to close it in a second, and reached out with his other. Noro padded over to him and smelled his outstretched fingers before licking them.

"Good girl. Okay—come on."

Everett grabbed her by the collar and led her across the living room. The last thing he needed was for her to get out in the middle of some sort of confrontation with her owner and take a piece out of him. As he passed the coat hangers by the front door, he spotted a red leash and grabbed it. Hooking it to her collar, he took her outside and handed the end of the leash to Hailey.

"What the hell is this?"

"Will you put her in my truck? Then meet us out back."

"What's going on?" Marie asked. Her eyes were wide and concerned. "That's a lot of blood, Ev."

"I know. Come on."

While Hailey took Noro out to his truck, Everett led Marie to the back door and opened it. The sight that greeted him almost brought him to his knees.

A large section of snow had been melted away by the flames, revealing earth that was now scorched. A melted red gas can sat at the very edge of the near perfect circle, and at its center were three skeletons.

Two were clearly human, the other likely a dog, all of them burned black. The words of Jonah's letter echoed on Everett's mind as he stood rooted in place.

You'll find the three of us in the backyard.

"My God..." Marie muttered, stepping aside as Everett rushed back into the cabin and out the front door. Descending the stairs two at a time, he found Hailey closing the door of his truck, and ignored her as she asked him a multitude of questions his mind couldn't begin to comprehend.

Opening up the driver's side door, Everett leaned in and grabbed his radio.

"This is Everett Bailey. I need back up and a forensics team out here on Prairie Way. I've got what looks like a murder suicide."

He only half listened to the response, really only understanding that help was coming. Behind him, Noro whined as she looked longingly at the cabin. Snow slowly began to fall again, drifting through the grey sky anew, and Everett tried not to think about the letter's warning.

Taking a steadying breath, Everett climbed back out of the truck and slammed the door. He made his way back up to the house where he found Hailey standing in the middle of the bloody room. The sounds of vomiting drifted in from outside, followed by cursing. When Marie appeared in the doorway, she looked like she was about to faint.

"Oh, shit," Everett managed. Luckily, Hailey was faster to react than he was. She reached her EMT partner in seconds, grabbing her before she could fall.

"You okay, Marie?" Hailey asked, her tone low and kind.

"I've never seen anything like this."

"Here, sit by the fire," Hailey said, helping her over to one of the kitchen chairs. "Do you need anything to drink?"

"Water, please."

Hailey nodded, crossing to the kitchen.

"Hey, Hailey, this is a crime scene..."

"I know that," she said angrily. "I'm not going to step in anything or touch anything. I'm just getting the jug of water."

Everett wanted to protest, but didn't. He could see how bad off Marie was, and knew that the right thing to do was to make sure she was okay. Instead of arguing, he simply nodded.

The cold air from outside sucked the heat from the still warm stove out of the cabin quickly, so Everett busied himself with closing both the front and back doors as Hailey made her way back to Marie with the jug of water.

"Here, drink this."

Marie took it from her and brought it to her lips, chugging it. As Everett returned, she offered it to him. The bitter taste of vomit was still present in his mouth, and it became all he could notice as he looked at the jug.

He took it from her and took a long swig from it, savoring

the taste. As he swallowed, something caught in his throat and he began to choke. Handing the water to Hailey, he raised his fist and coughed violently into it.

When he pulled his hand away, a small, white shape moved across his clenched fingers, blindly searching.

It got into his dog, then it got into him, then got into me.

Acknowledgments

Whew. That was... a wild ride.

I know what some of you are probably thinking – what happened to the guy that wrote those other three horror novels? The truth is that I'm right here, working away at more stories that tackle similarly difficult themes that many of us can relate to. I know I can! And even Noro had its moments, with Jonah dealing with the immense guilt that consumes him over his wife's death.

But Noro is, by and large, a *true* horror novel. There's not much of a "literary bend" here, as I like to say. This is a novella about two neighbors, their dogs, and an alien parasite that gets into one of said dogs. The scene where Doc meets his demise is one of the hardest things I've ever written, barring some scenes in The Man Behind the Door that were specifically inspired by my own father. I felt sick as I finished, but I also knew the moment that Doc's muscles started moving sporadically that I had something that felt truly special—and terrifying.

I hope you all enjoyed the novel despite some of the more graphic moments dealing with Doc. This novella was an experiment for me, written on the heels of another novella that has yet to see the light of day outside of my Patreon.

Speaking of Patreon—this story wouldn't be what it is without your support. Rosina, Rhonda, Molly, Autumn, Jody, Alex, Coretta, Lisa, Osk, and Jay, the belief you have in me pushed me to write (and continue to write) new, exciting, and different things. Without you all, Noro would never exist.

Patrick Reuman of Wicked House Publishing – it feels weird to shout you out here in a book I took somewhere else, but I don't think this would be happening without your continued support. WHP has taken me places I never imagined, and I can't wait to release my next book with you guys in September.

Now on to the man of the hour: Dan Franklin. Dan, being the incredibly nice guy that he is, agreed to take a look at this mean little novella after my continued success with Wicked House Publishing. It was all pretty non-committal, and he made no promises. I didn't expect much to come out of it, but here we are. This book is as beautiful as it is because of his editing and hard work to bring it together. From the cover to the interior art to the fine-tuning of the prose, Dan is a living legend when it comes to making a book the very best it can be. Thank you for bringing me into the Cemetery Dance family. All the love, brother.

To Cemetery Dance themselves, for being a cornerstone of the horror publishing world. Ever since I first saw a CD on a Stephen King book nearly a decade ago, I dreamed of seeing that same logo on my own book. I never imagined it would come to fruition.

To Blaine, Brandon, Clay, Andrew (Najberg and Van Wey), MJ, Ben, John, Jon (without the *h*), Patrick, L.M., Jay, Leigh, Megan, and everyone who runs Books of Horror (RJ, Hans, Tiffany, Heather, Erin), I can't thank all of you enough for everything you've done to help me along.

To the readers: I'm sorry for killing Doc. I mean that.

To my beautiful wife and amazing (and batshit insane) children: I love you with all of my heart. Every sacrifice and every kind compliment enables me to follow this once silly and unachievable dream of mine. Thank you all, so much.

Lastly, I want to thank Dave Simons. If you ever happen to read this, I hope you know that the kindness you showed me as a teenager was a foundational building block for getting here. Every book you loaned me of Stephen King's was one more that fed the fire of wanting to do this. Now, here I am. Thank you, man.

Truly.

William F. Gray, 2024

About the Author

William F. Gray is an author living in West Virginia. He has released three novels and a novella, has appeared in anthologies, and currently works full time as a pharmacy technician at an independent pharmacy while raising his son and daughter with his wife. In his free time, he enjoys outings with his family, reading, and playing music. His favorite authors are Clay Mcleod Chapman, Josh Malerman, Blaine Daigle, and Philip Fracassi.

patreon.com/williamfgrayfiction

facebook.com/williamfgrayfiction

amazon.com/stores/William-Gray/author